A Life:

Phase One (A Novelette) and 28 Short Stories

A Life:

Phase One (A Novelette) and 28 Short Stories

by Martin Green

iUniverse, Inc.
Bloomington

A Life: Phase One (A Novelette) and 28 Short Stories

iUniverse books may be ordered through booksellers or by contacting:

iUniverse
1663 Liberty Drive
Bloomington, IN 47403
www.iuniverse.com
1-800-Authors (1-800-288-4677)

ISBN: 978-1-4759-7905-3 (sc)
ISBN: 978-1-4759-7906-0 (ebk)

Printed in the United States of America

iUniverse rev. date: 03/12/2013

FOREWORD

I'm primarily a short story writer, as testified to by having over 250 short stories published in online magazines. But every so often even a creature of habit such as I am feels like doing something new. A few years ago I wrote a longer piece which turned out to be a fictionalized memoir called "One Year in Retirement." Back then I said that a longer work would be time-consuming and that at my age I didn't have much time left to spare. This is even truer today. I cheated a little this time by using a lot of material I'd used in short stories for this longer work, which turned out to be a novelette (30-50,000 words, by dictionary definition).

In the novelette I followed the doings of a young man who returns home to New York City after service in the Army, which was after he'd finished college. His goals are to find a job, find a girl, and find a place of his own to live. I called the novelette "Life: Phase One," although perhaps it should be "phase three" or phase four," considering childhood, college and maybe the Army as preceding ones. But I looked upon those preceding phases as being preliminary and thought establishing his own life with a job, a girl and his own living place was really the "Phase One."

I knew from writing the fictionalized memoir that doing a longer piece of writing was quite different from dong a short story. Instead of having to deal with two or three characters you had to keep track of maybe a dozen, which included making sure you got their names right all the way through. With a short story often one sitting was enough to get it done. With a longer work you had to re-enter the imaginary world you were creating every time you resumed writing. Literary pundits tell you that in a longer work your principal character should not remain static but should undergo some development over the course of the story (just as real people presumably develop over the course of their lives). I didn't set this as one of my goals in writing "Phase One," but I think that my protagonist did change from what he was at the beginning, young and inexperienced, to how he ended up, older, more experienced, possibly a bit more tough-minded. The reader will have to be the judge.

One of the things I dislike in a novel (or novelette) is when some characters simply drop out of the narrative and remain unaccounted for. I tried to let the reader know what happened to the persons who played a part in the protagonist's development, although they were not there at the end. I believe that Somerset Maugham, a favorite writer of mine, said that having the protagonist get married was a satisfactory way of ending a novel. I've ended my novelette this way. I'd say that getting married was at once the end of one phase of life and the start of another. Phase Two would include starting the family, in most cases buying a house with all of its attendant problems (failing heat and air-conditioning systems, appliances that stop working, a leaking roof, mowing the lawn, fighting off weeds and crabgrass, dealing with falling fences, etc., etc.), the struggle to advance in the job so that increased income covers increased expenses, and, above all, coping with all of the problems that come with having children. A common feeling in Phase Two is looking back at how pleasant life was in Phase One.

At any rate, what follows is one example of a Phase One. I'll remind readers that it's fictional.

Roseville, California
February 2013

LIFE: PHASE ONE

Coming Back From the Army

On a June day in 1954 a young man stood on the deck of a troopship bringing soldiers back from Germany to the United States. The sun rode high in the sky and glinted off the placid waves. The young man's name was Danny Stein, who'd been drafted after college during what was then called the Korean police action but which anyone involved in it, especially those who'd fought in it, knew was a war. Behind him the deck was filled with soldiers, playing cards, shooting dice, talking, happy to be liberated from below, where most had been seasick the past few days while an unseasonable storm had rocked the little boat. The fresh sea air felt like a tonic after being imprisoned below with the smell of urine and vomit.

Danny was for the moment oblivious to all of the activity on deck. He knew he should be happy to be getting out of the Army after two long years and he was. But his dominant feeling was anxiety. During those two years he had no need to worry about the future. He went where the Army sent him, did what the Army told him, most of the time anyway. It was, he'd later realize, the closest he'd ever come to living in the moment. Now he wondered what lay ahead of him. He knew he'd be returning to his old bedroom in his parents' apartment in the Bronx. Then what? The first thing would be to get a job. Then he'd want to get a girl. And he'd want to move to his own place. Maybe the second thing would be to get his own place, and the third thing to get a girl.

He didn't know it then, but at times when he faced a turning point in his life he'd make it a habit of looking out at large bodies of water and think about what he should do. Perhaps subconsciously the sight of something which had been there long before and would be there long after put whatever problems he had in perspective. At any rate, the waves of the Atlantic rolled off into the distance while he wondered about his future.

Most of the troops on the ship were New Yorkers like himself and many were what today we call African-Americans. At the time he thought of them as Negroes or colored guys. Before everyone got seasick they'd tried to outdo one another with stories of what great deals they'd had in the Army: the cushy jobs, the money they'd made selling American cigarettes, the German girls they'd taken to bed. Outwitting The Man, he supposed they'd call it. He wondered what kind of future awaited them back in Harlem, where most of them lived.

Danny supposed he'd had a good deal in Germany. After being drafted, he'd gone to Camp Kilmer in New Jersey and then to basic training at nearby Fort Dix. He'd been a little worried about getting through basic as he'd dislocated his right knee playing handball two years before, but although his knee ached a little after long marches he'd managed all right. Danny was a little below middle height and stockily built like his father. He didn't consider himself an athlete and had been about average in the street games that a kid growing up in the Bronx played. But for some reason he was good at handball and had captained his high school team for two years. He wasn't fast enough for singles so had played doubles and he and his partner had lost only one game in that time.

Looking back at Fort Dix, this was one time he hadn't always done what the Army had told him. Toward the end of basic, everyone was marched to a big auditorium in the center of the camp. They were going to get their future assignments. Danny sat next to Dave Fineman, who was a few of years older than him, and who had a PhD. Fineman was a funny kind of guy, who one weekend had risked a court martial for being AWOL by taking off to see an exhibit at the Metropolitan Museum of Art. Sure enough, he'd been caught without a pass when he came back Sunday night, but their sergeant, Threadgill, another funny kind of guy, had only given him company punishment.

"What do you think?" asked Danny when the crowd had settled down.

"It's a lottery. They probably put everyone's name in a big barrel and pulled them out at random." Fineman didn't think too highly of the Army.

"Come on," said Danny. "We're college graduates. Why did we take those tests at Kilmer? We'll get something where we can use our education." This showed how naïve about the Army Danny was at that time.

"Wait and see."

A captain stood on the stage in front and began calling off names. It was strangely like a high school graduation ceremony except that the assignments could have serious consequences. He called off names for cooks' school, truck drivers' school, clerk-typists' school, and other schools, then he said everyone else would go to field linesman school. Danny's name hadn't been called, meaning that he was among the many going to field linesman school. He couldn't believe it.

He had only a vague idea of what a field lineman did. He pictured someone climbing up a pole in a field and doing something with a wire on top of it. One thing he did know, field linemen were always sent to Korea. So, added to his picture of a figure on top of a pole, were bullets whizzing all around.

"How can they do that to me?" he asked Fineman.

"What did you expect from the Army?" Fineman himself, with his PhD, had been assigned to I&E, Information and Education, where he'd wind up with a teaching job.

David realized that he may have been a college graduate but to the Army he was just another body. "What should I do?" he asked Fineman.

"Maybe you can get into I&E."

"I only have a bachelor's degree."

"So what. In the Army, you can teach as well as anybody."

This sounded reasonable. "I'll have to talk to somebody," Danny said.

"I know somebody in I&E. He's only a PFC but you can try him."

The next morning as they were marching off to somewhere or other Danny spoke to Sergeant Threadgill. Threadgill was a trim light-skinned Negro who did everything quickly and well. He had a contemptuous manner, but seemed as contemptuous of the officers as he was of the new recruits. He also always knew what was going on. Danny told Threadgill that it was important for him to get over to I&E.

"What's the matter?" said Threadgill. "Too educated to be a field lineman?" Yes, he always knew what was going on.

"No, but I'd just as soon be doing something else."

Threadgill gave Danny a long, hard look. Rumor was that he'd seen action in Korea. Finally he said, "Okay, I'll give you one hour." He scrawled something on a piece of paper. "Here," he said, handing Danny the paper. "If anyone stops you, show them this."

Danny quickly walked to the I&E building and asked to see the PFC whose name Fineman had given him. Luckily, he was there. Danny told him he was a college graduate and planned to be a teacher and asked if there was any chance of being assigned to I&E. The PFC had gone to Danny's college in New York and, like Fineman, had a PhD. He seemed doubtful but took Danny over to a lieutenant, who looked more like a college professor than an officer, The lieutenant also seemed doubtful but told Danny he'd see what he could do.

Danny waited nervously while several phone calls were made, aware that his one hour was quickly going by. Finally, the lieutenant came over and told Danny he couldn't swing I&E for him. "But we can get you into clerk-typist school," he said. Clerk-typist school. Danny thought. Well, it was better than being a field lineman.

"Okay," he said quickly. "Thanks. That would be great." He shook hands with the lieutenant, thanked Fineman's PFC friend, then ran back to find his platoon.

In later years, Danny sometimes thought about Threadgill, wondering if he'd gone to Vietnam and, if so, what had happened to him. He was pretty sure that Threadgill would have survived. He also sometimes wondered what would have happened to him if he'd gone to Korea and was pretty sure he wouldn't have survived.

In the event, Danny had gone to clerk-typist school, then his class had been dispersed to various places, most, like Danny, to Europe. There he'd been dispatched to Seventh Army Headquarters in Stuttgart, Germany, working in the office of the Colonel in charge of Ordnance. The Colonel was another interesting character Danny met in the Army. They'd had a curious relationship, Danny later thought. He wouldn't say the Colonel had been his mentor (did they even knew that word way back then?) but he knew the Colonel considered him a hopeless college kid (maybe in the same way Sergeant Threadgill had) and he took a certain amusement in instructing Danny how to cope with Army life.

On Danny's last day he had a little talk with the Colonel. "So you're leaving us?" the Colonel said.

"Yes, sir."

"Think you're ready to be a civilian again? No more free room and board. No more Army to take care of you."

"I'll manage," Danny said.

"That remains to be seen." The Colonel lit a cigarette. He was a man in his forties, ruggedly built, handsome, with jet black hair, a square jaw and piercing blue eyes. He used a cigarette holder and Danny emulated him, not on base but when he went on leave, although instead of looking sophisticated and all-knowing, Danny thought he probably looked foolish puffing on his holder. "Do you have any plans?"

"To sleep for two weeks." Whatever their relationship, Danny could say things like that to the Colonel.

"And after that?"

"I guess I'll have to look for a job."

"I hope you'll remember some of the things I told you."

"I remember them all. Survey the terrain. Always have a way out. Don't be impulsive. Weigh all my options. Keep my mouth shut. And don't be a wise-ass."

The Colonel smiled. "Well, maybe you'll stand a chance after all."

Maybe he hadn't had a cushy job; the Colonel was an exacting taskmaster. But it could have been worse. He'd made a few good friends on the base, notably Gil Wexler, a University of California grad, who'd introduced him to German beer and also a few German girls. In addition, he'd been able to see a bit of Europe, including two weeks just before leaving when, courtesy of MATS, Military Air Transport Service, he'd flown to London, then flown from there to Paris, then gone by train to Florence and Rome. The Colonel had lent him the money for the trip. Still, at the time he considered that the two years he'd had to spend in the Army were, if not totally wasted, two years he could have used to get a start in life, whatever that start might have been.

Danny's reverie was interrupted by a raspy voice saying, "Don't think too much." It was Stanko, still another interesting character he'd met in the Army. Stanko was a little taller than Danny and a little thinner. He was dark, with black hair and narrow brown eyes that usually looked sleepy but Danny knew that Stanko was always on the alert and could move quickly, like a cat, when he wanted to. He was a born and bred New Yorker, a kid who'd grown up on the East Side. He's enlisted for a three-year hitch and, when Danny arrived in Stuttgart, was working in the base warehouse. Stanko had the reputation of being an operator and when on Christmas day Danny had pulled guard duty he'd contrived to get him a bottle of whiskey afterward. And one time when somebody in the PX had hassled Danny about being a "Jewboy," Stanko had stepped in with a switchblade and that had ended the incident. Danny didn't closely question what people meant when they called Stanko an operator.

"I won't. How are you doing?" He knew Stanko had been playing poker nonstop during the voyage and was sure he'd been winning.

"Not bad."

"Ready for civilian life again?"

"Damn right. No fat-ass officers ordering me around."

"Some weren't so bad."

"Yeah, I know that colonel you worked for was okay. You were lucky."

"So I guess you're not going to re-up?"

Stanko laughed. "You're fucking A I'm not."

"Do you know what you're going to do?"

Stanko shrugged, a New York shrug. "I got a couple of irons in the fire."

Danny figured he probably had. He wished he could say the same.

"C'mon," said Stanko. "It's chow time. Wouldn't want to miss another great meal."

Two days later Danny and Stanko were again at the ship's railing as it sailed into New York Harbor. The Statue of Liberty came into view. "There's the old lady," Stanko said. "It won't be long now, we'll be in the city, New York, there's no place like it."

"No, I guess not."

"Boy, first thing I'm going to do is have a pastrami on rye."

"That sounds good."

"And a New York broad. Those German chicks don't compare."

Danny nodded. He'd been to London, Paris and Rome but thought New York was the greatest city in the world. As the troopship pulled in he began to feel excited at the prospect of being in New York again. Mixed in with the excitement though was a fear of what would come next. As the song that wasn't yet written would put it, could he make it there? Well, he'd find out. Maybe things would work out all right.

*   *   *

New York: Looking for the Job

It was a Monday morning in August. As on the previous three Monday mornings, Danny was on the subway going from the Bronx to downtown Manhattan. He wore his old graduation suit, blue, with a red necktie his mother had bought him. In his inside jacket pocket was the section of the New York Times help wanted ads that he'd clipped out for this day's search. He was in pursuit of his first goal on returning from the Army to New York, finding a job.

He'd waited until nine to leave to avoid the worst of the morning's rush but even so all the seats were taken and he hung onto a strap, swaying with the motion of the train. The air inside the subway was stale and Danny wondered why no one thought of opening a window. Air-conditioning in the subway was a long ways off. He looked around at his fellow passengers, some other young men in suits, older men in work clothes like his father, who was a plumber, mothers with their kids clustered around them, a few young women. He noticed one sitting down, her legs crossed, in those pre miniskirt days not revealing anything much. Still, she was attractive and her legs were nice. Already one or two of his aunts had asked if he wanted the phone number of a nice girl; a nice Jewish girl it went without saying. He'd told them he wasn't ready to call any girls yet. First, he had to get a job.

Crossing into Manhattan, the train plunged underground like a burrowing monster. The noise became a roar. The vibration became worse and people had to cling to their straps. After stops at 125th and 86th streets the train pulled into Grand Central Station. Time to get off. Danny was pushed along with the other passengers getting out the door, which was already closing as if to cut off their escape. He climbed the stairs out into the street and took a breath of air. It wasn't really fresh but it was better than the subway. Most of the help wanted ads in the Times were from employment agencies. He'd already been to several on his previous trips downtown. He'd marked down the ad showing the most jobs to visit first; it was a few blocks north of Grand Central. Well, here go again, he said to himself.

The streets of Manhattan were as usual crowded. People of all sorts walked past quickly and purposefully, men with briefcases, women carrying large handbags, a few attractive young women with cases, maybe models carrying their portfolios. Everyone seemed to have a destination to go to. Danny noticed a number of young men carrying the Times folded to the classified section, obviously job-seekers like himself. This is why he'd clipped out the ads and had them in his inside jacket pocket. He didn't want to advertise that, unlike the people with jobs, he had no particular destination, except of course an employment agency.

This one was on the third floor of a medium-sized office building. Despite its large ad, it turned out to be of only moderate size. Like the ones Danny had been to before, you filled out an application form, gave it to a bored-looking girl, then sat in a waiting room with other young men, although there were also a few older ones this time, well-dressed, their shoes gleaming, wearing wedding rings, consulting papers from their briefcases, or maybe pretending to consult them. Danny wondered what had happened to bring them to a place like this.

Finally, Danny's name was called and he was allowed to enter the inner office. The interviewers, men in their thirties, were seated at shabby-looking desks. The whole place, Danny thought, looked shabby, like an enterprise with no chance of success. One of the thirtyish men waved him over. He had a round face, plump cheeks and snub nose, giving him the look of a pig or baby. He didn't ask Danny to sit down but Danny sat anyway.

The pig-man, still ignoring Danny, glanced through what Danny assumed was the application he'd filled out. Finally, he looked up and said, "Liberal arts major, huh? Pretty good grades. No business courses. That's not going to do you much good. Why not go in for teaching? You could probably end up being a college professor. That would be your best bet."

A college professor. Danny thought of Mr. Rolfe, the college professor whose assistant Danny had been for one semester. Mr. Rolfe was then about 30 years old. He had a photo of a pretty woman and a little girl on his desk; these were his wife and daughter, he'd told Danny. He was writing his Ph D dissertation on Plato; his relevance to the modern world, as Danny recalled it. He had to finish it by the end of the term or lose his teaching job. Danny was to do research in the library and typing for him.

It hadn't taken Danny long to see that Mr. Rolfe was a long way from being finished. As the term neared its end, Mr. Rolfe had dark rings under his eyes; he was obviously not getting much sleep. His writings became more hurried and, it seemed to Danny, incoherent at times. On Danny's last day Mr. Rolfe said he was nearly finished and just had to pull it together . . . Danny assured him he'd make it, but in his own mind he didn't think he would.

Danny had given a lot of thought to just this option, becoming a college teacher, but he'd already been set back by his two years in the Army. Then there'd be three more years in graduate school and even then he might wind up like Mr. Rolfe. Plus there would be the expense and he didn't want to rely on his parents' support. No, he'd weighed all his options, as the Colonel had told him to, and decided he wasn't going back to school and he wasn't going to spend the rest of his life on a college campus.

Danny didn't intend to go into all that with the pig-man. "I've decided I don't want to go back to school," he said. "I want to start doing something right away."

The pig-man shook his head. "That's too bad. I don't think we have anything for you."

"What about all those jobs you advertised, college graduates, no experience needed."

"All of those are filled. We'll keep you on file and call you if anything comes up"

"Sure," said Danny. The interview, if you could call it that, had gone the same way as all of those he'd had before with employment agencies. Somehow those many jobs advertised had vanished into thin air. He wondered if anyone was ever called back; he doubted it. He went back out through the waiting, still filled with applicants and the same bored girl, who, as Danny left, called out someone else's name.

It was now mid-morning. Out on the street, it was already hot and humid. Danny took off his jacket and loosened his tie but still felt hot. He looked at his clipping. Another employment agency was close by. He had no hopes but thought he might as well try it. It couldn't be any worse than the last one. At first, he couldn't find the agency, then saw that it was in an old building on a side street. He climbed up a winding flight of stairs; at the top was an office little larger than a broom closet. It was filled with cartons and cartons of—what, applications of people long since dead. Behind a battered desk sat an old woman with tangled gray hair, a cigarette dangling from her lips and a wild look in her eyes. He was wrong; this was even worse than the first agency. Danny said, "Sorry, wrong place," and fled back down the stairs, the old lady's voice calling, "Don't go away, sonny. Don't go away."

Back on a main avenue, now sweating, Danny located a coffee shop. He stepped inside and thankfully it was air-conditioned. He ordered a glass of milk and a slice of apple pie. The milk was cold and the pie good. While he ate and cooled down, he thought about his employment agency experiences. When he'd first looked at the Times help wanted pages the ads made it seem that there were hundreds of jobs waiting in New York City and all you had to do was pick the one you wanted. Evidently this was not so. These were phantom jobs. Then why did the agencies print and pay for the ads? Was it just to get people to come in so they'd have something to do? Were the agencies all part of a giant conspiracy, and if so, what was the conspiracy about? One thing was for sure, no more employment agencies for him. They were a waste of time. He looked at his clipping from the Times again. There was one ad, much smaller than the rest, for an agency that said executive placement. The address showed it was just one block away. Okay, just one more.

The waiting room of the executive placement agency was an improvement over the other agencies Danny had been to. The chairs were comfortable, the lighting was good and the receptionist, instead of looking bored, was smiling. He'd filled out an application and given it to her with his resume attached. There were only two other men, both older, waiting; they didn't look as desperate as the older men he'd seen earlier that morning. After only a five-minute wait the smiling receptionist led Danny into what looked like a real office. A man of about 40, stood up behind his desk, introduced himself as Brian Richards and asked Danny to sit down. "I've looked over your resume," he said. "So you were over in Germany with the Army?"

"Yes."

"I assume you were drafted. How'd you like the Army?"

"I wouldn't make it a career, but it wasn't too bad. I got to see some places I wouldn't have otherwise."

"And you were a liberal arts major but now you want a job, not teaching?"

"That's right. The other agencies I've been to seem to think that's a crime."

Richards smiled. "It a handicap but not a crime. How are your writing skills?"

"I think they're pretty good. I'm also pretty good with numbers."

"Did you take any statistics courses."

"Yes, one. It was pretty basic."

"Any prospects so far?"

"None. The other agencies I've been to act as if I'm hopeless."

"Well, most companies prefer a business major. There are a lot of young men like yourself looking for work right now, and of course New York City is a very competitive market. Also, our economy is in a bit of a downturn."

"So you think I'm hopeless, too."

"No, only that it's probably going to be difficult. And you're a first-time job seeker so there's that old conundrum: employers want experience but how do you get experience if you don't get that first job?"

"What about all those jobs those agencies advertise, college grads, no experience needed.

"I'm afraid those exist only in the imagination of those agencies."

"Then why advertise them?"

"Their aim is to get as many applicants on file as possible. There are some jobs out there and maybe they'll be able to find someone in their files to match one of them."

"I see. So where does that leave me?"

"To tell the truth, we don't take on first-time job seekers. That's why we call ourselves an executive placement agency. But I went to the same college as you so I wanted to see your resume. If I may offer a few suggestions, did you have any summer jobs while in college, or even in high school?"

"Yes, I did. One of my uncles has a wholesale button place and I worked summers in the stock room."

"Put that in. Also, put down anything you did in the Army that you might be able to use."

"I worked in an office, typing and filing."

"Good. Typing is a skill you can always use."

"So you think I should re-do my resume?"

"Yes. And I'd forget about those so-called employment agencies. Make a list of companies you'd like to work for, then contact them directly."

"How do I find those companies?"

"Do some research. Go to the library. You must have done that when you wrote papers in college."

"Okay, I can do that."

"Good. I'm sorry I can't give you any more help, but keep at it. And I will keep my eyes open for you and let you know if I see anything."

With that, Richards stood up and they shook hands again.

Back out on the busy street, Danny thought, well, that didn't do much toward getting a job, but he still felt encouraged. He'd try Richards' suggestions and hope they'd help his search.

*   *   *

After Labor Day, Danny, still unemployed, made his first visit to the Central Park handball courts. He took the subway to 86th Street, then took the local two stations up to 103d Street. Before going into the Army, he'd played at the MacCombs courts, next to Yankee Stadium, and the center of handball activity in the Bronx. He was a regular in the weekend money games. His partner was a tall, gangling Negro of indeterminate age called Slim, who was said to have been a boxer. This could very well have been true as he was missing most of his front teeth. Whatever the case, Slim was one of the best players at MacCombs Dam. For some reason he'd taken a liking to Danny and they'd become a doubles team. Danny's role on the team was to play steadily while letting Slim, with his strong wrists, hit killer after killer. They almost always came out ahead in the money games. But Danny had found out that the MacCombs Dam courts had been torn down, to make way for a highway that, as far as anyone knew, was never built and never would be. As for Slim, someone said he'd been killed one summer; the rumor was that he'd run numbers and run afoul of some mobsters. In any case, he'd disappeared.

Danny had heard that the Central Park courts had a fair amount of activity and so here he was, dressed in an old shirt and warm-up jacket, a pair of his old Army khaki pants and the tire-soled sneakers he used to play in at MacCombs Dam. Stuffed in the back pocket of his pants were his old well-worn handball gloves, held together by a couple of thick rubber bands. As he walked to the park, a smartly-dressed girl strode quickly past him going the other way, another one of those New York girls, he thought, like the ones he'd seen downtown, confident, poised and, to him, unapproachable.

Danny came to the edge of the park and started up the path leading to the courts. The trees in the park, all green, were a welcome relief from the city streets. The worst of the summer heat was over; it was warm but not humid. When he reached the courts he saw a small knot of people watching one of the games. He joined them and watched for a while. It was evidently what passed for a money game at Central Park. The best player was a thin, dark curly-haired guy who looked Italian. Danny asked one of the spectators and found out his name was Mike. His partner was an older man, totally bald, who just tried to return the ball. One of the players on the other team made a big production of serving the ball, bending over so far his nose almost touched the ground and contorting his body into a pretzel, but when he finally served the ball had nothing much on it. His partner was a big loudmouth who hit the ball hard but didn't know where to place it. If that's all the Central Park courts had to offer, thought Danny, he had nothing to worry about.

After a while, Danny got into a game on one of the other courts. His partner was a tall blondish guy about his age who was enthusiastic but not too well-coordinated. They played two men about 40 years old who weren't that good but played a steady game and seemed sure they were going to win. They were ahead at first while Danny got warmed up and took turns making smart remarks to Danny's partner, whose name was Alan. Danny gathered they'd played against Alan before and usually beat him. When Danny opened up a little and served out the game, Alan was overjoyed and came over with a big smile to shake hands. Their opponents demanded a return game and this time Danny, now fully warmed up, saw to it that he and Alan led all the way.

By this time it was mid-afternoon and as they toweled off Alan said to Danny, "You play a terrific game."

Danny shrugged and said, "I'm pretty rusty."

"I bet you play a lot."

"I used to."

Danny told Alan about being in the Army and returning to New York. Alan revealed that he lived with his parents near the park and was going to NYU law school. His father was an attorney. Danny had the impression that his family was pretty well off. Alan asked if Danny would be coming to Central Park again. Danny said, "Yeah, probably next weekend." Alan smiled and shook Danny's hand again. He said he'd wait so they could be partners again.

*   *   *

Danny had done what Brian Richards of the executive placement agency had suggested. He'd revised his resume, composed a cover letter and made a list of companies to go to directly. So he found himself going into the lobbies of tall office buildings and studying directories. He rode up elevators and invaded reception rooms, asking to see someone about a job. Usually, he was directed to a personnel office but occasionally he got in to see some company officer, a low level one, who'd tell him that they might have something sometime. Danny would leave his resume and say that he'd call back. He felt that at least he'd established a contact and that he was doing something productive.

Going into these buildings and talking to the people in them gave Danny a funny feeling. All of these other people were on the inside. Somehow they'd managed to penetrate the mysterious business world. They were the ones who moved so confidently through the streets of Manhattan. They all, even the lowliest clerk among them, had their places in the scheme of things. Meanwhile, he was the outsider. Maybe that's why his fellow job hunters in the employment agency waiting rooms wanted to keep to themselves. They didn't want to acknowledge that they too were among the outsiders.

Two weeks after he went to the Central Park courts Danny secured his first interview with one of the companies he'd gone to. The company was in one of the new glass buildings which seemed to be springing up like weeds everywhere in Manhattan. Danny took the elevator up to the twentieth floor and entered a reception room filled with ornate cups and plates, giving the impression that the company made rare china although in fact it produced soap flakes, cleaning products, and toilet paper. The receptionist greeted him, made a phone call, then told him that Mr. Walker would see him in a few minutes and returned to the paper-backed romance novel she was reading.

Danny sat and waited, first reading through a company magazine, then looking through a couple of news magazines. After half an hour a youngish man, blonde and cheerful-looking, came out and introduced himself as Mr. Walker. "Sorry to keep you waiting," he said. In a tone that indicated he really wasn't, "but I got busy. You know how it is."

Danny nodded to show Walker that he knew how it was and followed him back to a modest office with no window. Walker seated himself behind an absolutely clear desk, waved Danny to a chair and picked up some papers, one of which was Danny's resume. The first thing he asked was if Danny had any business experience; he didn't see it on his resume. When Danny had to say No, but he was a quick learner and was ready to start at the bottom and work his way up, Walker asked why Danny wanted to work for this particular company. The truth was that Danny just wanted to get a job, any job, so that he could get started in his post-Army life. Aloud, Danny said he'd always admired the company's products, mentioning the soap flakes and cleaning products but not the toilet paper. Walker then asked about his Army duties and Danny told him he'd become an expert typist and ran a Colonel's busy office for him.

This seemed to exhaust Walker's curiosity or maybe he really was busy because he next led Danny down a corridor to a small cubicle and left him there to take some tests, which he said were standard for anyone applying for a job with the company. The first was an intelligence test, which Danny found easy and finished quickly. Next was what appeared to be some kind of personality test. At the top of the first page was a statement that there were no correct answers to the test, that you should just answer honestly. This immediately sounded a warning. Danny looked through the first few questions. They asked things like if you preferred to play football or go to an art gallery, if you were ever attracted to members of your own sex and if you sometimes contemplated suicide. Danny thought that if you honestly answered Yes to those last two questions you weren't likely to be hired.

The third and final test was even more invasive than the personality test. It asked about the applicant's political and religious beliefs and other matters more personal and private. For a moment Danny considered writing on the test that these were none of the company's business, but he'd come this far and for all he knew all companies had these kinds of tests. He answered so that it appeared he was the blandest person possible with no extreme views of any kind. He wondered if somebody had sold the company a bill of goods, making it seem that it could pick the best candidates on an absolute scientific basis. Later on, Danny would read that this was the time of the "organization man," in which all large companies wanted employees who would fit into their particular mould. And still later, such tests would be considered an invasion of privacy and couldn't be administered.

Danny took the tests and, as instructed, gave them to the receptionist, who looked up from her romance novel, smiled and told him the company would be in touch with him. Somehow Danny wasn't hopeful. It was still early in the day so he walked to the Army office, which was close to Times Square. Like all ex-G.I.'s, he was a member of what was called the 52-20 club; the Army generously doled out $20 a week for 52 weeks. In between his downtown visits to employment agencies and then to companies, Danny had been stopping into the Army office to collect his weekly check.

The office was really a large barren room where you lined up, as you did for everything involving the Army, to collect your check. A couple of military policemen stood around nervously as if expecting the unemployed veterans to start a riot. On this day, Danny heard his name called in a familiar voice. He turned around and, sure enough, there was his friend from Seventh Army Headquarters, Stanko, now dressed in flashy civilian clothes. "Hey," Stanko said. "How come you're here? Don't tell me a college boy like you hasn't landed a job yet."

"It's not that easy," Danny said. "But how come you're here?"

"Hey," said Stanko, winking, "why pass up 20 bucks a week. Don't worry, I got a few things going. But they're under the table, know what I mean? Hey, if you're interested, I can probably get you in on something."

Danny recalled that on the personality test there was a question, Have you ever done anything dishonest? "No, I don't think so. But thanks anyway."

Stanko shrugged, as if to say, What can you expect from a college boy? "Okay, you want something legit, I get it. But how come it's so hard for a smart guy like you?"

"Well, one of the things making it hard is that I'm unemployed so don't have any work experience. The guys doing the hiring don't like that."

"Yeah, you need experience to get a job, but you can't get a job because you don't have any experience." In the future there'd be a book whose title summed this up, "Catch 22."

"That's about it."

"Okay, no problem. Here." Stanko handed Danny a card that said import/export on it. "Just say to call that number. I'll tell them you work for me and give you a great reference."

"But that would be lying."

Stanko gave Danny a pitying look. "Look, you're in the real world now. You have to do what it takes."

"I don't know if I can do that."

Stanko gave one of his New York shrugs and said, "Well, think about it. I'm here if you want."

*   *   *

Danny was an only child and the first one in his family to go to college. His high school grades were good enough so that he'd won a scholarship that paid for his tuition, then not the thousands of dollars that it later became. The money he earned working summers at his uncle's wholesale button place, plus his handball winnings, gave him spending money. His father was a first-generation American who'd been in the Navy after World War I, then had become a plumber. Danny had grown up during the Depression years and knew his parents hadn't had an easy time. His father had taken any job he could and had worked for the WPA at one time. It wasn't until World War II and defense work that his father had begun to earn a decent living. Even then he had to work out of town during the war and for some years afterward. Finally, New York City had a housing boom that he'd been able to come home and rejoin his family.

Now Danny still didn't want to ask his parents for spending money even though he knew they'd gladly have given him some. The money from the 52/20 club and the money he still had from his savings just about covered his expenses. He hoped that eventually he'd add some handball winnings to that. He went downtown almost every weekday. After making his rounds, he got into the habit of walking up to Central Park. He went to the zoo and occasionally walked up as far as the Metropolitan Museum of Art. He remembered that during basic training Fineman had risked going AWOL to attend a show at the museum. He found it calming to wander around the Metropolitan Museum, so different from that world of glass buildings, companies that gave would-be employees ridiculous tests and employment agencies that advertised non-existing jobs.

But after a while, Danny's mother started questioning what he was doing all day. Why hadn't he be able to get a job yet? Maybe he should become a teacher. Maybe he should go back to school. Or he could get a job with his uncle at the button place. Danny's father said she should leave him alone; he'd be all right. Just be patient.

*   *   *

On Danny's second visit to the Central Park handball courts, his new friend Alan, true to his word, was waiting for him. They played and won again. Danny also watched the money games again and his initial impression was confirmed: the players weren't in the same class as those at MacCombs Dam. After a few more weeks he felt he was ready and got into one of the money games. He and his partner lost but it was close. They played again and this time won. After that, Danny became one of the regulars in the money games. They didn't play for as much as at MacCombs Dam but he started taking home 20 to 30 dollars a week. That, plus the $20 a week from the 52/20 club was enough for his expenses with a little left over. In those days, the subway cost a nickel, two hot dogs and a soda at a deli was a quarter and a dinner at a pretty good restaurant could be had for two or three dollars.

Although Danny no longer played handball with Alan, they became friends. They usually met for dinner once a week at one of the cheap, but good, German restaurants in Yorkville. Alan told Danny about how hard law school was and about how hard it was to date a girl in New York. Danny told about his adventures in job-hunting. They agreed that they'd like to move out of their parents' places and have a place of their own. Danny said that if he ever found a job maybe they could find a place together.

On a Saturday in late October Buddy Wolfe came to the Central Park courts. He worked for the city as a fireman, but his profession was handball player. He'd been one of the best players at MacCombs Dam and the word was that he now played at the Brighton Beach Club courts, home base for the city's top players every summer. The club closed after Labor Day so he was probably making the rounds of the other city courts, looking to pick up some easy money. He had with him as his partner a guy called Russ, who looked more like a football than a handball player, and an older smooth-faced man, Smitty, who acted as his manager. Since Danny, along with Mike Costello, were now considered the two best money players at

Central Park it was arranged that they play Wolfe and Russ. The odds against them were two to one. Their backers also wanted a spot of six or seven points.

While they argued about this with Smitty, Buddy Wolfe, staying above it all, warmed up and Danny watched him. Wolfe was about 30 years old and of no more than average height, but he moved about the court like a cat. He seemed to hit the ball equally hard with his right and left hand. Smitty didn't want to spot any points, saying Russ was just a marginal player and this would even things out. Everyone wanted to see Buddy Wolfe play and so finally they gave in and the game started.

It took only a few points for Danny to see that Russ was better than a marginal player; still, although he hit the ball hard he was erratic and prone to errors. The strategy was obvious; keep the ball on Russ's side of the court. The problem as that Buddy Wolfe was so fast that he could get over to return the ball on Russ's side and still get back to cover his own side. Besides this, his serve was so good, he could hook it to either side, that both Danny and Mike had a hard time even getting it back. And Russ was adept at getting his large body in front of the man on his side and blocking him out. Almost before anyone knew it, the game was over, 21-7. Danny's friend Alan came over to console him. "You played okay," he said, "but that guy is fantastic."

"He can be beaten," Danny said. It was something Slim would have said. Danny had no idea how it could be done.

There was a long discussion about a return game. After the one-sided first game Smitty had to relent and he agreed to a spot of six points. The odds also went up to three to one. The spot mattered as Buddy Wolfe and Russ got seven points on their first service game and then moved out to a 13-6 lead. When Danny and Mike finally got the serve, Mike served first and got two points to make it 13-8.

Danny moved over to the left side to serve. He'd been trying to serve to Russ but Buddy Wolfe played so far over that unless the ball was hit to the extreme right side of the court he could still return it. Danny decided to try something different. He edged over to the center and looked at Russ. But instead of serving to him, he hit it to the left just over the service line and also hooking it to the left. Wolfe was so fast that he got over but his return, with his left hand, wasn't as hard as usual and Danny was able to hit it through Russ to make it 13-9.

As Danny bent over for his next serve he saw that Wolfe had shifted slightly to cover his left. He served to the right but not to Russ, just far enough over to make Wolfe run to return it. The return was to Mike's side but, following the ball all the way, Danny moved over and killed the ball in the middle of the court. Both Danny and Mike were in front of Russ and he had no chance to get of getting to the ball. Wolfe was racing to cover his left corner and even he couldn't recover quickly enough.

Now Danny had a sequence of points in which he seemed to know exactly where to hit the ball and exactly where the ball was coming back. As the saying goes, he was in the zone. He saw the court in sharp focus, like a football running back who sees where all the defenders are. He alternated between his hook serve to Buddy Wolfe's left and making him go far over to his right. He moved to the return and hit the second shot either hard to Russ or angled it to Wolfe's left, carrying him far out of the court.

Somehow Danny knew when Buddy Wolfe would cover his left and when he'd try to cover the rest of the court. For this stretch, Danny was so intently focused that he was unaware of the spectators yelling as he and Mike tied the score and then took the lead. When Wolfe made a miraculous save to end Danny's serve it was like coming out of a trance. He asked Mike what the score was. Mike told him they were ahead 20-13. Damn, he thought, one more point and they would have won it.

Russ served and couldn't do anything. Then Buddy Wolfe served. Earlier he'd been smiling and joking with the crowd. Now he looked grim. His serves came like bullets and he was all over the court. In what seemed like only minutes, the score was 20-20. Wolfe served for the game. The ball came to Danny. He guessed the ball would hook to the right and managed a decent return. Wolfe went for a kill shot. Mike dove and got it back up but the ball was a set-up. It was on Russ's side of the court. Wolfe moved over to put the ball away. Russ stepped in front of him. Later, Danny speculated that the shot looked so easy that Russ thought that for once he'd be the hero. He hit the ball as hard as he could. The shot went two feet wide.

Mike served, just an average serve. Buddy Wolfe moved over and went for a kill from the long line to end the point right there. The ball hit an inch in front of the wall. Buddy Wolfe was human. He'd missed his kill shot. Danny and Mike had won, 21-20. They immediately ran to each other and hugged. The crowd converged on them and pounded them on their backs. Alan pushed his way through and told Danny, "Great game."

Danny gave him an answer Slim always gave after a close game, "We had it all the way." Smitty disconsolately handed over their winnings. With the three to one odds Danny pocketed over a hundred dollars. Afterward, Danny walked with Alan out of the park. Alan asked how the job hunt was going. "Pretty much the same," said Danny. "My resume is all over the place but nothing doing. It's getting to be depressing. Maybe I should become a professional handball player."

"Don't worry, something will come up."

The next week Danny received a phone call from a man who said his name was Brian Richards. It took a few seconds before he remembered that Richards was the guy he'd seen at the executive placement agency. Richards asked if he was still looking for a job, then said he'd heard there might be an opening in an advertising agency, Levy, Namm and Singer He knew the agency's research manager Jack Grossman and Danny should call his secretary and make an appointment for an interview. Danny thanked Richards and immediately made the call. The secretary told Danny to send in an updated resume and made an appointment for him to come in the next Monday.

Danny didn't know anything about the advertising business and he'd never heard of Levy, Namm and Singer. He knew that advertising had a certain glamour to it. A book and later a movie called "The Hucksters" had come out, the movie starring Clark Gable no less, and advertising was made to seem exciting and full of drama. Danny hadn't seen the movie but he'd read the book. He went to the library and found out that Levy, Namm and Singer had a major cigarette client and, strangely, that the soap flakes and toilet paper company where he'd interviewed was another client. He looked through some other books and thought that he wouldn't seem completely ignorant, but he wasn't very hopeful.

Danny hadn't known what to expect but without filling out any applications or taking any tests he was led into a small office whose sign said: "Jack Grossman, Research Manager." Grossman was a man in his early thirties, short, fleshy and already balding. His sleeves were rolled up and his collar open. He looked busy and harried. An ashtray on his desk was filled with cigarette butts. The office smelled of smoke. Grossman stood up and shook Danny's hand. He held Danny's resume and was about to speak when his phone rang. He answered and said something which sounded to Danny like "submerge the target market under the median strata." He put down the phone and, still standing, said to Danny, "Your resume looks okay. Brian says you're good with numbers and Mr. Stanko says you're one of his best salesmen. That's good. Can you start tomorrow?"

Danny was so startled that he was almost speechless. He managed to blurt out, "Uh, yeah, sure."

"Okay," said Grossman. "My secretary will take you to Personnel and you can fill out all that crap." His phone rang again and he waved Danny out of his office.

*   *   *

Danny walked up Madison Avenue to Central Park. Once again he had to make his way among all those people hurrying along, the men with their little attaché cases, the women with their huge bags, all having someplace to go. And now he was going to be one of them. The next day he too would have a place to go. Instead of being on the outside, drifting like a ghost through the streets of Manhattan, he'd be on the inside. He reflected a little about the difference between the handball courts and the business world. At the courts it didn't matter who you were and who you knew. At MacCombs Dam, there were judges, lawyers and even a movie critic, also people like Slim who might have run numbers. What counted was how well you played. He felt a little guilty about using Stanko's phony reference, but in the business world, as Stanko had said, you had to do whatever it took. When he reached the park he saw one of those little food carts that were all over New York. He felt that he had to celebrate with something so he went over and bought a salted pretzel. Then he went into the zoo.

*   *   *

Danny became aware that Jack Grossman was hovering over his desk. "Got those figures yet?" It was a question that Danny, in his three months working in the Research Department of the Levy, Namm and Singer advertising agency, had heard very often. Grossman was perpetually worried and whatever the figures were he was in constant fear that he'd get them too late. This past week was even worse than usual as the Research Department was dedicating almost all of its time to the agency's cigarette client, which, Danny had learned, had the second-most billings. Tops was the soap flakes, cleaning products, toilet paper, etc. company, which everyone there called the Giant.

The government had come out with a report that cigarette smoking was detrimental to one's health, something which the cigarette companies were then vigorously disputing. Still, cigarette sales were down and there were rumors that their client might be looking around for another agency. Losing a client, Danny had quickly learned, was the worst thing that could happen to an ad agency.

"I have them for the ten largest SMA's," Danny said. "I gave them to Zee to graph them. I thought that would make it easier for the account execs to understand."

Al Zimmerman, known to everyone as Zee, had the desk next to Danny's. Danny had established a reputation as being good with numbers. Zee was good at graphing.

"Hmmm," said Goodman. "Okay, good idea. Keep on with the rest of the SMA's. We need them quick."

"Right." SMA's were Standard Metropolitan Areas. This was one of many research terms Danny had picked up; market share, sales to ad dollars ratios, moving averages and trend lines were some of the others.

The Research Department was a large unadorned room where a dozen analysts, as they were called, labored away at metal desks, seated on uncomfortable metal chairs. Each desk had on it a large clunky calculator of the kind everyone used in those days so that the room was always noisy. This was before the age of computers and cubicles. Only Jack Goodman, as Research Manager, had his own office, about the same size as a cubicle today but somewhat more private. One other person had a private office, Sarah Cohen, who had a degree in psychology and who conducted consumer surveys. These, Danny was told, were supposed to find out people's likes and dislikes and why they bought or didn't buy various products. It was an area that sounded interesting, much more so, than adding up or dividing numbers and he hoped to learn more about it. Danny supposed Sarah Cohen was part of the Research Department, but she reported directly to Bob Decker, Vice President in charge of research for the agency. Decker was said to be a prodigy who amazed everyone with his research ideas and had become a vice president in his twenties. It didn't hurt that he was also Singer's nephew.

Danny labored until lunchtime, then as usual Zee called out that it was time to leave the salt mines and they got their coats, joined by two other analysts Henry Fox, another Bronxite, and Amy Brown, who was married and lived in Queens. It was one of the coldest winters in the history of New York; luckily, there was a delicatessen only two blocks away and they were able to get there without being frozen. Every time they went there Danny remembered Stanko's telling him the first thing he was going to do when they got back from the Army was have a pastrami on rye. He'd called Stanko after getting the job at Levy, Namm and Singer to thank him and had called him two or three times since, offering to buy him a lunch in appreciation but Stanko was always busy, with what he never did say. Danny had also called Brian Richards, the placement agency guy who'd told him about the job opening, and thanked him. Richards had wished him luck and asked him to report any job openings at the agency he might hear of.

The lunchtime conversation of the four young analysts was mostly about the cigarette account and the rumors circulating around it. Their main concern was if the account might go to another agency and, if so, then what about their jobs? Amy Brown was the only analyst not worried about this. Like most young women back in the 1950's, she expected to start a family and was only working to save money so that she and her husband could buy a house. Henry Fox was a different story. He was the most openly ambitious guy Danny had ever known. His immediate ambition was to take over the Research Department, calling Jack Grossman a washed-up old man. Danny had several times caught him, when Grossman wasn't there, sitting in the Research Manager's office, swiveling around in a chair as if taking stock of the kingdom he expected to rule over.

After lunch, they returned to find Jack Grossman pacing around the room, looking even more anxious than usual. "Where you guys been?" he asked. "I just got a call from Decker. They need those figures at the end of today."

"We were at lunch," said Zee. "We have to eat sometime."

"Okay, okay. Just get back to work. And no afternoon break."

They watched Grossman go into his office; he slammed the door closed, hard.

"That guy's going to have a heart attack," said Zee.

"Yeah, and I'll be here to take his place," said Fox.

Danny went back to his calculator. By late afternoon, the numbers were swimming before his eyes. And all to sell more cigarettes, which the government said were bad for your health. Almost everyone in the agency smoked, their account's brand of course, and the smell of cigarettes was everywhere. Danny was glad he'd stopped smoking when he'd gotten back from the Army No one then knew about second-hand smoke. Danny was finally finished at seven o'clock. He handed his work to Grossman, still in his office with piles of paper all over. No one else was left in the Research Department. He put on his coat, walked to the subway and prepared for the long subway ride back to the Bronx. One good thing about working late, the evening rush was over. He found a seat and closed his eyes, too tired to even read the copy of Advertising Age, the industry bible, that he'd brought from the office. As always he wished he made enough for an apartment in Manhattan. Maybe when he got a raise, which was supposed to be when he'd been there for a year. If he was still working there, that is. He thought about the cigarette company rumors. When he'd finally landed a job, he'd thought that he would no longer have to worry about that aspect of his life any more. Now he wondered, not for the first time, about his future in the advertising world, if he had one.

*   *   *

New York: The Girl

Danny was again on the subway, this time riding from his parents' apartment in the Bronx to his cousin Ben's in Brooklyn. Danny's mother was the one who'd urged him to go to the party. She'd been relieved when he'd gotten his job with Levy, Namm and Singer. Now she'd no longer have to explain to her mah-jong friends why her son, a college graduate, didn't have a job. She'd rather that he'd gone into a profession; still, she had no problem referring to her son the advertising man. The next step in his homecoming would be to find a nice Jewish girl. The two or three girls whose numbers she obtained for him hadn't worked out too well. One had that flat nasal New York voice that Danny hated. Another had giggled all the time. Maybe he'd meet somebody he liked at the party.

It was now spring in New York. The coldest winter was over. The cigarette company scare at the agency was over, ancient history. Work had resumed its normal course. The Research Department devoted most of its time to the Giant, with its many products that sold everywhere. Danny's main job was still crunching numbers, but he was beginning to understand what they were all about. He'd expressed an interest in consumer surveys and Sarah Cohen had loaned him some books on sampling and probability. She'd also had him coding questionnaires. Danny thought she was pretty old, at least 30. She wasn't pretty but she had a forceful presence, with strong features and a square jaw. She could be brusque, but underneath he thought she was a nice person.

The party was in the basement of his uncle's house. This was the uncle who owned the wholesale button business where Danny had worked summers as a kid and where his mother had wanted him to get a job when he couldn't seem to get one anywhere else. His cousin Ben was about a year older than him and was studying to be a dentist. No button business for him.

A dozen or so young people were already in the basement when Danny arrived. The boys seemed to be in a separate group from the girls. His cousin introduced him around. Three of the guys, like his friend Alan, were in law school; one was in medical school and two were accountants. They asked him what he did. No one had heard of Levy, Namm and Singer.

One of the accountants said, "I hear you can make a lot of money in advertising."

Danny thought of his meager starting salary. "I'm in research," he said. "The pay isn't too great."

After this, the others lost interest and drifted away. They all seemed to know one another and there was a lot of talk about how much money a lawyer or a doctor could make. The girls seemed to be talking about friends of theirs who were getting married. His cousin put some records on the phonograph; this is what provided music in the time before tapes, CD's and iTunes. The boys and the girls started to mingle and then to dance. This left him out. The high school he'd gone to had been all male, the same with his college. He'd never been to a dance or learned how to dance.

When Danny first came in he'd noticed a slender brown-haired girl with a serious face and gray eyes. Now she was dancing. The stack of records seemed to be endless but finally the music stopped and, plunging ahead before his shyness could overcome him, he went over to her. "Hi, I'm Danny Stein," he said. "Ben's cousin."

"Oh, yes. From the Bronx. I'm Marilyn Gold."

"From Brooklyn?"

"That's right." In answer to his questions, she told him she'd graduated from Hunter College the year before and was now teaching school. During the last summer she'd been to Europe, a graduation present from her parents, with a girl friend. Danny told her about being stationed in Germany and about managing to travel to several other countries while he was there. They talked a little about the places both had been. He liked her voice; it was soft, unlike the usual harsh New York tone. Then the music started again and one of the law students carried her off to dance. He didn't get another chance to talk to her the rest of the evening.

The next day Danny called his cousin and got Marilyn Gold's phone number. "She's a nice girl," said Ben, "but I think she's going out with some one, an engineer. He's in grad school somewhere."

"Oh," said Danny. Just his luck. He almost threw away the phone number but then thought, what the heck, I'll give it a try anyway. It took him a week before he gathered up his nerve, then he called. If nobody was there or if one of her parents had picked up the phone that would have been the end of it, but it was Marilyn who answered. He started by saying, "You probably don't remember me. I'm Ben's cousin Danny."

"Yes, I remember you, from the Bronx."

This threw Danny off his stride for a moment as he'd prepared a speech explaining who he was. "Uh, yes, from the Bronx. Uh, how are you?"

"I'm fine. How are you?"

"Uh, I . . ." Danny decided he sounded like an idiot. "Look, I really liked you. Can I take you out this weekend?"

"Oh, I'm sorry. I'm busy this weekend."

Did she already have a date? With that engineer? "What about next weekend?"

"All right."

All right. Wait a minute; did he have a date? He asked her address. She told him and told him the nearest subway station and how to get there from the station. Yes, he did have a date. He arranged to be there at seven o'clock. Before she hung up she asked if he was an accountant.

"No, I work in an advertising agency."

"Oh. Well, then you can tell me all about advertising."

*   *   *

"So how's the big advertising man?"

Stanko had finally met him for lunch at the deli near Danny's agency. They were both having pastrami on rye. "Not so big."

"Yeah? How much they paying ya?"

When Danny told him, Stanko laughed. "Jeez, when they take out taxes I bet it's not much more than the 52/20 club."

Danny agreed. "You still making some dough playing handball?"

"Not right now. I couldn't play over the winter, too cold, then I had bursitis, in my right shoulder. And my right knee, the one I dislocated when I was a kid, started to bother me."

"Too bad. So how's the job going?"

"Pretty good, I think. I'm learning something. I don't feel like a rookie any more."

"How're the people there?"

"You know, the agency is pretty much like the Army. In the Army, everyone has a rank, officers only associate with other officers, noncoms with other noncoms and of course officers and noncoms would never associate with an enlisted man. The same thing, the account execs are the top rank, then the creative people, then the media buyers and I suppose we research people are at the bottom."

"Sounds about right. Well, you can't get any lower so you'll have to fight your way up."

"I guess so. The worst thing though is that everyone, from the account execs on down, is afraid."

"Yeah, of what."

"Of the clients. If one threatens to leave there's a panic." Danny was voicing some of the things he'd been thinking about advertising, not the glamorous occupation outsiders thought it was. "Anyway, how's the import/export business?"

Danny thought that he'd get the usual evasive answer, but Stanko had a surprise. "I'm not in that business any more. I'm on Wall Street."

"Wall Street?"

"Yeah, one of those big outfits. I'm just a messenger now, but I'm learning stuff, just like you. That's where the money is."

Danny congratulated Stanko. He had no doubt Stanko would fight his way to the top. He insisted on paying for their lunch. "If it wasn't for you I probably wouldn't have gotten the job."

"Okay," said Stanko. "Tell those meatball clients to go screw themselves."

"I wish we could."

*   *   *

Marilyn lived with her parents in an apartment even further out in Brooklyn than Danny's uncle's house. When Marilyn opened the door to let him in he saw that she was more attractive than he remembered. Her hair was long and light brown, almost blondish. Her gray eyes were large and luminous. He noticed that her hands were slender and sensitive-looking. She led him into the living room and introduced him to her parents, waiting there to give him the obligatory inspection. Marilyn's mother was both shorter and stouter than her daughter. Marilyn evidently took more after her father, who was a tall light-haired man. "What is it you do?" the mother asked him at once. When Danny told her she looked dubious. "That's not a very steady business, is it?" she said.

"Some people have been there a pretty long time," he said, wondering if that was true.

Mrs. Gold shook her head, still dubious. "Better a young man should have a profession." This sounded familiar; his mother and Marilyn's belonged to the same club.

Marilyn saved him from having to reply by saying, "We'd better get going if we're going to see a movie."

Danny had studied the movie section of the Times and luckily had found a theater just a few blocks from where Marilyn lived. The latest Alfred Hitchcock, "Rear Window," was playing. Danny wondered as they sat down if he should hold her hand but couldn't decide and then he got caught up in the film. But afterward, as they walked back to her apartment talking about how much they liked Hitchcock, he did take her hand and she asked him in for coffee.

The apartment was dark and Danny supposed that Mr. and Mrs. Gold had gone to bed. He and Marilyn continued their discussion of movies, then switched to plays they'd seen. This led Danny to talk of his visits to London while he was in the Army, where tickets were so cheap and so easy to get he'd gone to see a play every night. Marilyn hadn't been to England during her European tour but had been to France, Italy and Spain. They compared their experiences in Paris, which they both thought to be the most beautiful city in the world, and Rome, which he'd liked but she hadn't.

She became more animated as they talked and when she smiled it lit up her normally grave face. Before Danny knew it two hours had gone by and it was past one o'clock. "I guess I better be going," he said. When he asked if he could see her the next weekend, she said she was busy but could see him the weekend after that.

At the door, Danny kissed her, at first tentatively but then firmly on the mouth. He walked to the subway, feeling pleased with himself; the first date had gone well, he thought. When he looked back on it he had to smile at how chaste it had been. A decade later, in the sixties, they'd probably would have smoked some pot and had sex right then and there.

At that late hour the only subway still running was a local. Danny sat in an almost empty car while the train made its interminable journey into Manhattan, stopping it seemed every two minutes. But for the moment he didn't mind. During all the time he was in Europe he'd imagined coming back to New York City. Even though London had affordable theaters and Paris was beautiful there was no city like New York. Look at Broadway and Fifth Avenue, Rockefeller Center, Times Square. And New York had the Yankees, the Giants and the Dodgers. He remembered the letter he'd had from his Army friend Gil Wexler, now back in California, urging his to come out to San Francisco. No, San Francisco might be nice and the rents cheaper, but how could it compare? New York was the center of everything. It was exciting, things hummed, anything could happen. And after that long period of unemployment, now he had a job in New York which might turn out to be a good one and now maybe he had a girl. He recalled the day he'd looked out at the ocean from the troopship. Possibly things would turn out all right after all.

*　　*　　*

He should have known better, thought Danny. The week after his big date the bombshell fell on Levy, Namm and Singer; Levy was leaving. After a morning of rumors, which had Levy taking all of the agency's big clients with him and everyone being fired, Jack Grossman came out of his office to talk to his little group of researchers. "I don't know what you've heard, but the agency's not folding. Levy's taking a few of our accounts but not the big ones. We still have the cigarettes and the Giant. The word is that as long as we keep them we should be okay."

Danny wanted to ask about promotions but decided not to. He'd learned in the Army to keep a low profile. He'd find out anyway in a few months. As they broke up, Henry Fox muttered, "I'm going to update my resume right now."

"Don't panic" said Zee, always optimistic.

Amy Brown said she wasn't worried; she was planning to leave at the end of the year.

"Yeah, if we're still around by then," said Fox.

Danny kept his thoughts to himself. Back at his desk, he remembered what Marilyn's mother had said, that advertising wasn't a very steady business. She may have been right. And just when he was starting to feel comfortable.

*   *   *

Shortly after that Danny's friend Alan produced a bombshell of his own. Danny and Alan were still having an occasional dinner together at one or the other of the inexpensive German restaurants in Yorkville. A while ago Alan mentioned he'd started seeing a girl he really liked. Danny hadn't paid too much attention; Alan was always seeing a girl he really liked and shortly after they'd break up. Now Alan announced the unthinkable, he was getting married.

"But you've only known her for a month," said Danny.

"Two months, but she's the one." Alan went on to extol the virtues of Clarice for the next half hour. "My father's going to set us up in an apartment as a wedding present. I get out of law school in June so then I'll start making some money."

Danny knew Alan would be going into his father's law firm. It helped to come from a family with money. There went his plan for sharing an apartment with Alan after he got his promotion. Of course he wasn't sure any more about getting a promotion so maybe it didn't matter. Aloud, he said, "Congratulations." To himself, he thought, why get married when you were just getting started? Then he thought of Marilyn. Where would that lead? Well, it was way too early to start worrying about that. But he had a feeling he'd be seeing a lot less of Alan from then on.

*   *   *

Danny was in Marilyn's living room after another one of their movie dates. They sat side by side on the living room sofa. They'd finished the coffee Marilyn had made. The apartment was quiet but Danny knew that Marilyn's mother and father were in their bedroom. It was late and possibly they were sleeping, but Danny felt that they, or at least her mother, was laying awake and listening to what was going on. It was getting to the end of summer and they had progressed, it was progress to Danny's mind, to having what would probably be called cuddling, in which they'd have long kisses and Danny would attempt other things but Marilyn would never let him go too far. With her parents almost next door in their bedroom he didn't think he could press her. Still, Danny thought, it was progress.

Danny had been seeing Marilyn throughout the summer, although she'd still tell him that she was busy on some weekends. He wondered if she was seeing someone else, that engineer his cousin had mentioned, at those times. He'd learned that Marilyn had lived in Brooklyn all her life, just as he'd lived in the Bronx. She had an older brother, married with two sons, one evidently very sickly. The brother and his family also lived in Brooklyn and Marilyn visited them often. She also baby-sat the sons. She liked children, which was why she'd become a teacher.

They broke off their kiss and Marilyn asked how things were going at the advertising agency. Since the panic after Levy had bolted things had pretty well settled down, although there was always an undercurrent, Danny felt, of fear running under all the busy activity, fear of something else happening and people losing their jobs. "I'm helping the researcher who does consumer surveys," he said. "She's letting me help her prepare the questionnaire for the next survey. It's pretty interesting."

"She? So she's a woman. Do you like her?"

Danny had to smile. Could Marilyn be a little bit jealous? "She's older, at least 30, and she's pretty tough. Nobody messes with her."

"But she must like you."

"I don't know. She likes me staying overtime to help her. The Research Department is spread pretty thin. She wants an assistant but they won't hire one so I guess I'm it."

"But you shouldn't be working overtime without pay?"

"I'm still hoping to get that promotion."

"I hope you do."

Danny took her in his arms and they kissed again. He fondled Marilyn's breasts. That was as far as he'd progressed.

Riding the local back home, Danny wondered, not for the first time, what other couples in New York City did to be able to go further. They could hardly do it in her parents' apartment and they certainly couldn't do it in his parents' apartment. He knew from what his fellow soldiers in the Army had told him that in other places it was done in the car. But in New York City who had a car, nobody he knew. He didn't even know how to drive. He needed to have his own place. For that he needed the promotion. Things seemed about back to normal at the agency so maybe he'd get it.

*   *   *

The next Monday Bob Decker, the seldom seen Vice President in charge of Marketing, amazed everyone by suddenly appearing in the big research room. Decker usually communed only by passing his directives down through managers. Everyone gathered to hear what he had to say. After spending five minutes to light his pipe, he finally spoke. His message was that the Giant was looking around for other agencies. The departure of Levy was nothing compared to this. If the Giant left that would mean the end of the agency, and, everyone's worst fear, the end of all their jobs. What Namm and Singer had to do now was to put together the next year's campaign in record time and knock the Giant's eyes out so it would stay. Decker told them this would mean working late hours and on weekends. He knew he could count on them because this was a matter of life and death.

As soon as Decker left and Jack Grossman returned to his office, the researchers shared their reactions. Henry Fox said that he'd already updated his resume, done after Levy had left, and would now waste no time in getting it out. Even the normally optimistic Zee was gloomy. He said he'd think about it; the Levy scare had blown over and maybe this would, too. But, as Decker had told them, this was a lot more serious. Amy Brown said that if they started firing people she'd volunteer to leave. Danny once again kept his thoughts to himself. There went the promotion. And when would he be able to see Marilyn?

The next day everyone in the Research Department got his or her assignment. Danny's was to go through the Giant's sales and advertising figures for the last ten years. It was Decker's idea, said Grossman, to give them an historical perspective. This was in addition to his work helping Sarah Cohen with her consumer surveys. As Decker had told them, they were asked to come in that weekend. Danny called Marilyn and told her about what had happened. She was immediately worried about his job. "Do you think it's true, if that one client leaves, the agency will have to close?"

"Yeah, I think so. That one client bills more than all our other clients combined. But they're not gone yet. I just won't be able to see you until the emergency is over."

"We can talk on the phone. I want you to keep me up to date. Maybe everything will work out, then we can celebrate."

"I hope so."

The next Monday afternoon while Danny was busy going through large binders of numbers his phone rang. It was one of the agency account executives wanting some information about another client right away. Danny told him he was in the middle of a job for the Giant and that he'd get back to him the next day. A few minutes later Jack Grossman called Danny into his office. "Close the door and sit down," said Grossman. He sounded upset. Danny wondered what was up.

"I just had a call from (he mentioned the name of the account executive who'd called Danny.) He wants me to fire you, immediately."

"I said I'd call him back. I couldn't just drop everything."

"Danny, when an account exec wants something you do drop everything."

"That's ridiculous."

"Maybe, but that's the way it works."

"So what happens now?"

"I told him we couldn't fire you because we needed everyone we had. But I want you to get that information and call him back right now. And tell him you're sorry."

At six that day Danny and Zee took time off for a quick meal at the deli, paid for by the agency, before going back for another two hours of work. Danny told Zee about having to apologize to the account exec. "Yeah, Jack's right," said Zee. "In advertising, account execs are the masters and lowly researchers are the slaves."

"But that's not right. All the account execs do is schmooze the clients. We dig up the facts that our advertising needs."

"The account execs keep the clients happy and it's the clients who count. Anyway, we have to jump when an account exec calls, they have to jump when a client calls. Say, you still seeing that girl who lives in Brooklyn?"

"Yeah, although I haven't seen her since we started working overtime."

"You must really like her to go all the way out to Brooklyn."

"I do like her."

"Have you, you know, done her yet?"

Danny was a little shocked by this question. "No, we haven't had a chance to do anything."

"I know what you mean. Thinking of getting married?"

Danny was even more shocked by this question. "Married? No, I'm not ready to get married yet."

"Yeah, but what about her?"

"We better get back to work."

During the next few weeks Danny called Marilyn several times on the phone. "I miss you," he said.

"I miss you, too. When will you find out?"

"Pretty soon, I think. I'll let you know as soon as we do." It occurred to him that maybe he should say, "I love you." But did he? Somehow this business of getting a girl was not as straightforward as it seemed when he first returned from the Army.

At the end of October, with the fall changing into winter, the Research Department finished all of its work for the Giant, two days ahead of the deadline. Danny called Marilyn to let her know he was finally free on weekends. And he had a surprise. The agency had rewarded everyone in the Research Department with two tickets to the "Pajama Game," a Broadway musical that had opened earlier that year. His tickets were for the next weekend, a Sunday matinee. He half expected her to say she was busy that weekend but she said that was great. She'd come downtown and meet him so he wouldn't have to ride the subway all the way out to her place.

The next Sunday was crisp and sunny. Danny got out of the subway at Times Square. He stood on a corner while people hurried by on all sides, then he saw Marilyn across the street. She saw him at the same time and her face was lit up by her smile. After not having seen her for so long, Danny was once again surprised by how attractive she was. He rushed across the street, causing cab drivers and other motorists to honk their horns at him, and they took each other's hands. "I'm glad to see you," he said. If he'd been any less shy he would have kissed her. They stood for a moment smiling at each other, then she took his arm and they went to the theater. Their seats were in the tenth row of the orchestra. Danny said he'd never seen a play from so close; his usual seat was in the balcony. Marilyn said neither had she; the seats were great . . . Feeling somehow triumphant, they enjoyed the musical.

Afterward, they had an early dinner at an Italian restaurant Danny had discovered, which served a six-course dinner at an incredibly low price, even for that time. He told Marilyn about all the ups and downs at the agency during the last weeks. He didn't tell her about the incident with the account exec who'd wanted him fired. "I think it's horrible," she said. "All that uncertainty."

"Let's not worry about it now. I really missed seeing you."

"I hope nothing else happens at your job."

After dinner, they took the subway back to Brooklyn. At that hour, the subway wasn't crowded and they sat side by side holding hands. Danny saw two or three older women smiling at them. When they arrived at Marilyn's apartment, her parents were still up. "I hear the place you work in might close up," said Marilyn's mother.

"We don't know yet."

She shook her head. "I've always said it's best to have a profession."

Danny and Marilyn had coffee in the kitchen while her parents watched television in the living room. Danny thought they'd never go to bed but they finally did and he and Marilyn went into the living room and sat on the sofa. They kissed and he sensed that she was ready to do more, possibly much more, but then she said, "We can't, not with my parents right next door."

It was almost too much to bear. Why didn't they live in some small town so that he'd have a car? Why did her parents always have to be at home when he was there? He thought he knew the answer to that one.

*   *   *

It wasn't until the first week of December that the employees of Namm and Singer were to learn if all the agency's work on the Giant's new campaign had been successful. Decker once again made an unprecedented appearance in the Research Department. Once again he fussed around lighting his pipe while everyone waited. Then he looked around at the anxious faces, threw out his hands and yelled, "We've won!"

There was a stunned silence, then cheering broke out. Decker said, "The Giant is staying. We're going to have to tighten our belts but the agency will survive. Now let's all get back to work."

When they got back to their desks, Henry Fox muttered, "Belt tightening. I bet that means no Christmas bonuses."

At noon, Danny had a surprise. Sarah Cohen came over to his desk and said, "Come on, I'm buying you lunch." She strode away and Danny had no choice but to follow her.

Outside the building, Danny asked, "Why the treat?"

"You've been a big help. You deserve it."

The restaurant she took Danny to was considerably nicer, and more expensive, than the places Danny was used to going. They were seated at a table by the window. A waiter came over and Sarah ordered for both of them. "Well," she said, "I guess we still have our jobs."

"Looks like it."

"How do you like the ad business now?"

"It's not dull. But I'll be glad when we get back to normal hours."

"Advertising is never normal," she said.

The waiter brought their meals, a salad for her and a small steak for Danny that was the best he'd ever had. While they ate, She questioned Danny about where he lived, where he'd gone to school and what he'd done in the Army. "And where do you want to go from here?" she asked.

"I really don't know," he said.

"Well, you have a knack for statistics, that's good. I don't know if you fit into the ad game."

"Why not?"

"Well, for one thing, you're too nice and proper."

Danny blushed. He didn't think of himself as especially nice and certainly not as proper. It was funny, he thought, Sarah Cohen had never shown any personal interest in him before. When they finished, she said, "Back to the salt mines. Or, we could take the afternoon off. Everyone will be celebrating. My apartment isn't far away."

Her apartment? Was she asking him there to . . . no, that couldn't be. "No, I think we should be getting back."

She smiled. "All right. See, I said you were too nice and proper."

Back at the agency, Sarah was right, not much work was being done. He thought a little about Sarah Cohen. She lived by herself. With her brusque manner, she had no friends at the office, none that he knew of. Like most young men of his age he was preoccupied with himself and seldom thought of others. He wondered if this seemingly self-sufficient woman was lonely. He shook off his reverie and decided he'd leave early, nobody would mind, and call Marilyn with the great news.

*   *   *

The next week brought more good news for Danny. Jack Grossman called him into his office, told him he'd been doing good work, and that he was getting a five percent raise. Danny was amazed and elated. It was only later that he realized that it didn't amount to very much in dollars. Still, it was something. At lunch, he had another surprise. Zee asked if he'd like to go in with him to rent an apartment. Like Danny, Zee wanted a place of his own. They did some calculations and figured they could just about swing it. They arranged to go apartment-hunting that weekend. "How do you think your folks will take it?" Zee asked.

"My mother won't like it. She thinks without her I'll starve to death and never have any clothes to wear."

"Yeah, same with my mother. Jewish mothers don't think their sons can leave home until they get married, then their wives will take care of them."

Wives? A quick image of Marilyn flashed through Danny's mind. No, it was far too soon to even think about getting married. But if he had his own place, even sharing it with Zee . . . well, he'd see what would happen.

*   *   *

Saturday night. The apartment was filled with young people, talking loudly, smoking, drinking, trying to make out. The place wasn't big and it was in one of the old buildings in Yorkville. But it had two bedrooms, a living room, a kitchen and a bathroom. Above all, thought Danny, he was no longer someone still living with his parents; it was a place of his own; well, his own and Zee's. Some Namm and Singer people were there, still in a buoyant mood after keeping the Giant. The others were friends and friends of friends. Danny caught sight of Zee in the crowd. "Hey, isn't this great?" Zee yelled. He seemed pretty drunk.

"Yeah, great," Danny yelled back. Marilyn wasn't there. Of course, he'd considered asking her, but then had second thoughts. He'd known there'd be drinking and other carryings-on. He'd only had a couple of drinks himself and, unused to alcohol despite having dome some drinking in the Army, was feeling a little light-headed. No, it wasn't the right place for her. Some girl he didn't know rubbed up against him and asked if he had a cigarette. He told her he was sorry, he didn't smoke. She immediately lost interest in him and whirled away. Another girl he didn't know suddenly kissed him, then she too whirled away into the crowd.

It was after midnight when he saw Sarah Cohen. "Hi, Danny," she said.

"Sarah, I didn't know you were here."

It wasn't exactly clear what happened after that, he'd had another couple of drinks by then and was really woozy, but it was clear that he and Sarah had gone into his bedroom, where coats were piled on the bed, and, as it's described today, had sex. Afterward, he told himself it was the party, the drinking, the feeling of sexual desire that filled the apartment; he couldn't have helped it.

It was almost noon when Danny woke up on Sunday. He had a headache and a sour taste in his mouth. He forced himself to get out of bed. The place was a wreck, empty bottles filled the kitchen, ashtrays were overflowing, furniture had been moved about, a large rip was in one chair. He opened the door to Zee's bedroom a crack; Zee was in his bed sleeping. Danny made himself coffee and got dressed. He had the coffee and a piece of toast. He put on a jacket, left the apartment and walked over to the East River. Not many people were about. It was cloudy and cold; the water was gray and looked cold, too. A few small ships were plowing along. Danny, hands jammed into jacket pockets, looked out at the river and tried to bring some order to his swirling thoughts. What would the Colonel tell him: survey the terrain, don't be impulsive, weigh all your options. He considered: Sarah Cohen, the ad agency, the Giant, the year ahead, Marilyn—it always came back to Marilyn.

He remembered the last time he'd walked to Central Park and had gone into the zoo. The place had looked dingy and rundown. The animals in their small cages had looked unhappy.

They reminded him of Jack Grossman in his little office. He pictured the scene at the agency when Larry Decker had told them they'd won, the cheering, the relief of having survived. It was nice but the same underlying fear would be there as before. The researchers would still have to kowtow to the account execs and the account execs to the clients. Henry Fox, and all the others, would resume pushing their way to the top, until the next crisis. Then it would start all over again. He shivered. The wind had become stronger. The Colonel had said to sleep on any decision. He would. He walked back to the apartment and started in on cleaning up the mess.

*   *   *

Danny arrived at Marilyn's apartment on a Saturday afternoon. It was another gray day; snow was forecast for later. They went into the living room and took their accustomed places on the sofa. It was a dark room, and quiet. Danny thought he could hear a clock ticking somewhere.

"I have something to tell you," he said. "I'm leaving New York. I talked with an old Army buddy and I'm going to San Francisco. I can stay with him for a while."

"But what about your job here? You got a promotion. I thought everything was all right."

"It is, for now. But I don't want to stay there."

"Why don't you get a job somewhere else?"

"It's not only that." He took her hands. "It's a lot of things since I came back. It's hard to explain but I feel I have to get out of New York."

"And us?"

"I think your mother was right. I'm not good marriage material right now."

She pulled away her hands and put them to her face. She was crying. A physical pain cut through him. Suddenly, Marilyn's mother was in the living room. She must have been in the kitchen and heard her daughter crying. "What's wrong?" she asked.

Danny stood up. "It's nothing. Marilyn will tell you. I better go now." He backed out of the apartment, seeing Marilyn still crying and her mother glaring at him, the young man who'd done something to hurt her daughter.

                                    *   *   *

When Danny told his parents he was leaving New York his mother's first response was that if he did he need never come back and she'd never to speak to him again. Her next tactic was to ask how he'd live, how would he get a job, what would he eat, who'd do his laundry. Danny's response was to say, "Ma, I'm not a little kid any more. My friend says I should be able to get a job there. The city is growing. They have places called Laundromats. I'll be okay." After much going back and forth Danny's father had said that there son was right, he was a young man and he was going to go anyway, so let him go. His mother grudgingly gave in.

On the day of his leaving, his mother said, "You'll call when you get there, right?"

"I will, Ma.

"And you'll write every week?"

"Sure, Ma."

"I don't know what's going to happen to you. Here at least you had a job. And a home. And maybe you'd marry that girl Marilyn in Brooklyn. Now you're going to God knows what."

"I'll be okay, Ma. I better get going or I'll miss the plane."

She hugged him. Like Marilyn, she was crying.

Danny took a taxi to LaGuardia airport. It was the first week in January and it was a typical New York winter's day, gray, cold and dismal. "So you're going to California?" the cab driver said. "You're lucky. You'll be basking in the sun while we'll be freezing our asses off here."

Danny boarded the plane, which looked incredibly small, and took his seat. He thought of what his mother had said; she'd summed it up very well. He was going out to God knows what. The seat belt sign came on. The airplane went down the runway and took off, going directly out into the ocean, then it gracefully turned and headed toward the unknown West.

*   *   *

San Francisco: Party Time

It was a Friday night and Danny was at another party. This one was at someone's apartment, a large one in Pacific Heights with a view of the Bay. In a way, it reminded him of the one and only party he and Zee had had at their apartment in Yorkville, made memorable by his drunken encounter with Sarah Cohen. The apartment was packed wall-to-wall with young people, friends of the host, or was it hostess, friends of those friends, people who had heard of the party and just come, no one really cared. It was a BYOB, bring your own bottle. The work week was over and everyone was letting loose.

Danny had been in San Francisco for almost six months. The first few weeks he'd stayed with the Cal Berkeley grad he'd met in the Army in Stuttgart, Gil Wexler, and three other Berkeley grads. They lived in an old rambling house in North Beach. Danny had become familiar with North Beach, home to many Italian restaurants and to the City Lights bookstore. He's also become acquainted with other young people in Gil's circle, which he thought of as the Berkeley gang.

Then, surprised by how easy it was after his experience in New York, he'd gotten a job with a small but highly respected research firm, owned by a man named Tommy Flowers. Gil, who'd become a reporter on the local newspaper, told him Tommy (everyone called him that) was a pretty well-known man-about-town. He also had political connections, his father having been a state senator.

Danny had obtained an interview by answering a newspaper ad. Tommy Flowers was unlike anyone he'd encountered in New York. He was a handsome man, in his forties or maybe older, it was hard to tell, with blonde hair and sparkling blue eyes. He wore a rumpled seersucker jacket and (his trademark, Danny was to learn) a red bowtie. They discussed Danny's experience with Namm and Singer, his reasons for leaving there and coming West, the mechanics of consumer surveys and ways of finding out what people wanted to buy. After only 20 minutes Tommy offered him a job. Danny thought that possibly his having worked in New York carried some weight in San Francisco. The salary, although not tremendously high, was more than he was making at Namm and Singer and, as rents were lower in San Francisco, Danny had shortly after moved into an apartment on Octavia Street, within walking distance of his office downtown if you didn't mind walking 20 blocks or so. Tommy also advised Danny to get a car, he would need it to get around. At the end of the interview, Tommy had said, "I envy you, a young man in San Francisco. I think you'll have a good time." So far Danny had been having a good time. He'd gone to more parties since he'd been in San Francisco than he had in the rest of his life, and that included weddings and bar-mitzvahs. He'd also drunk more alcohol than at any time in his life.

The party was in full swing. Danny circulated around, or tried to in the crowd. He occasionally saw someone he knew, one of the Berkeley gang, and exchanged a few words. Ruth Baker, who was Gil Wexler's girl of the moment, asked him about his job and about he was doing in his apartment. Ruth always expressed an interest in what Danny, the newcomer from New York, was doing. She had a way of smiling at him, half-maternal, half-flirtatious. She asked if Danny did any cooking and when he'd said he didn't said she'd have to come over sometime and show him a few recipes. Ruth was a tall brunette with a voluptuous figure and she was wearing a low-cut dress that revealed the tops of her creamy breasts. He had a momentary picture of Ruth standing in his apartment, then immediately blacked it out. He was sure she was just saying that anyway. After that, he talked to a few girls but none gave him any encouragement. Without thinking, he'd had several vodka tonics (he'd brought the vodka) and his mind was getting fuzzy.

He found an empty corner and looked at the party. Young people stood close to one another, talking loudly to be heard. Their voices taken together sounded like the buzzing of bees. Scents of perfume mingled with smells of liquor. An undercurrent of sex ran beneath everything. He saw Gil Wexler, in the middle of a group, talking and drinking, undoubtedly expounding on the latest San Francisco gossip he'd picked up. Gil looked as if he was pretty well smashed. Danny finished his own drink and decided he'd better not have any more.

After another hour or so, the pairing-off ritual started, signaling the party was coming to an end. Some guys and girls would leave together, others would leave alone. It was time to leave himself, although he didn't look forward to going back to his empty apartment. He'd gotten a letter from his mother that week saying that his grandmother had fallen and broken her hip and was in the hospital. She gave him the name and address of the hospital and said he should write. She also wrote that his cousin Ben's wedding was next month and added that she hoped she'd lived to see him get married.

He'd started pushing his way toward the door when Ruth Baker came up to him. "Do you have your car?" she asked.

"Yes."

"Good. Gil has passed out. Do you think you can give me a ride?"

"Sure." They went outside. It was dark and the San Francisco fog had already come in so that everything looked blurred. Danny found his car and they started off. He was about to ask Ruth for directions to her place when she said, "Why don't you stop at your apartment? I'm curious to see it."

"You'll have to walk up three flights."

"Don't worry, I can make it."

Danny turned on the lights as they came in. He was glad he'd cleaned up a little. He quickly gathered up some newspapers that were lying around as Ruth went into the kitchen. She looked into his refrigerator. "Just as I thought," she said. "Nothing here."

"I was going to do a big shopping tomorrow."

"I'll bet." She came back into the other room and looked around. "It's not a bad place. It would look a lot better with some pillows around and a few pictures on the wall."

"I'll talk to my decorator."

She had moved closer to him. Her big dark eyes glistened. Danny wondered how much she'd had to drink. Now she put her hand on his face. "You do need someone to look after you, don't you?" She leaned still closer and kissed him. In the car, Danny had wondered if Ruth had something more in mind than wanting to appraise his apartment but he'd told himself not to be a fool. Well, you never knew.

They sat on the sofa, still kissing. Incongruously, Danny found himself thinking of Gil Wexler and if he was still passed out at the party. Suddenly, Ruth stood up and stepped out of her dress, then slipped off her bra. Danny stared at the white rounded breasts he'd only imagined and never though to see. She put her arms around him and smiled her half maternal, half flirtatious smile. "Come on," she said. Afterward, she smoked a cigarette. Danny found a plate to use as an ashtray. She went into the bathroom and came out dressed. She wanted Danny to take her home.

When Danny returned to his place his thoughts were in a turmoil. They hadn't talked much on the drive to Ruth's place. He hadn't known what to say. He didn't know what she expected of him. At her door she gave him a quick kiss and then went inside. As he drove back, he thought it was lucky there was so little traffic in the fog.

He sat for a long time, trying to sort things out. It must have been the party, all that drinking, all that pairing off, the feeling of sexual desire in the air you could almost touch. He'd also felt in bed that Ruth was acting at least partly out of curiosity. She wanted to check out the new guy from New York. Maybe Sarah Cohen had the same kind of curiosity back in New York. Maybe, Danny thought, because he was too shy to "come onto" them, as the phrase was, girls wondered about him. He didn't know. He did know that Gil Wexler was his friend. It wouldn't happen again. At the same time, he couldn't help wondering how close Gil and Ruth really were.

Finally he went to bed. He couldn't get to sleep for a long time and when he did he had a series of confusing dreams. When he woke up he remembered only the last one. He was in New York. He'd gone downtown to Times Square. Across the street he saw a slender brown-haired girl. It was Marilyn Gold, the girl he'd left when he came out to San Francisco. Then he remembered he was meeting her to go to a play. She lived in Brooklyn and was meeting him downtown so he wouldn't have to ride the subway all the way out there. That was sweet of her. He started across the street but a crowd of people got in his way and he lost sight of her. Then he was awake.

He looked at his bedside clock. It was 10 AM. He got up, did his business in the bathroom, then went into the kitchen and drank some orange juice. He looked out the window. It was gray and overcast, the kind of day when the weatherman said the sun might burn through in the afternoon and it rarely did. The phone rang. When someone called on a Sunday morning it was usually one of the Berkeley gang. Maybe it was Gil, or maybe Ruth. He didn't pick up the receiver. The phone rang several more times, then stopped. He looked around the apartment. He'd give it a good cleaning. After, he'd go shopping, as he'd told Ruth he would. And he'd write that letter to his grandmother.

*   *   *

Tahoe

Danny was having a sandwich in the casino coffee shop when a girl came over to his table and asked if she could join him. The shop was crowded but Danny saw a few empty tables. The girl was in her twenties, probably his age, attractive despite her heavy make-up and tangled hair. "Sure," said Danny. "Sit down."

After taking a bite of her hamburger, she told him her name was Zelda White. "I was at the roulette table when you were winning all those chips," she said. Danny nodded. He'd thought she looked familiar. "You're lucky tonight," she said.

"It doesn't happen very often." He'd been playing roulette because he'd played it before at casinos in Europe. As he'd done then, he bet on the zero/double zero and it had come up several times so he'd finished ahead.

"Are you here by yourself?" she asked him.

"Yes."

"And you drove up from San Francisco?"

"That's right."

"To get away from something."

"Right again."

"I'm psychic, you know. I could feel you had something heavy on your mind."

"I do have something on my mind." He'd driven to Tahoe that afternoon on an impulse, feeling it would be good to get away for a while. Since the night Ruth Baker had come to his apartment he'd tried to keep away from the Berkeley gang, although that was hard to do. Gil Wexler considered him a friend and he would run into others in various places downtown. But he hadn't gone to any more parties. He still wasn't sure about what had happened with Ruth and what he should do about it.

After he'd arrived at Tahoe and checked into a motel, he'd walked down to the still incredibly blue lake. He'd been to Tahoe a couple of times before. One of the Berkeley gang's parents had a cabin there and they'd stayed overnight in it. He had the idea that the lake might have a calming influence on his mind. But although the lake did its part by being still and peaceful, his mind insisted on being in its familiar turmoil. Finally, he'd given up and gone to the casinos.

"I have a good feeling about you," said Zelda. "You have a mentor, don't you? If you follow his advice you'll find the right thing to do."

A mentor? How could she have known about the Colonel? "Maybe you *are* psychic," he said.

"Oh, I am, but I still haven't done very well at the tables."

"Your psychic powers let you down?"

"They're not always attuned to the flow. I'm afraid I've lost all my money. Do you think you can let me have, say, twenty dollars?"

So that's what all this had been leading up to. Danny felt disappointed. "That's not a lot to gamble with," he said.

"If my feeling comes back that's all I'll need."

"Well, okay." He gave her the money. She thanked him and stood up." Will you be here for a while?"

"For a little while."

"I'll look for you. With your twenty dollars, I hope."

"Okay." He was sure he wouldn't see her or his money again.

Danny finished his meal and walked around among the tables. He was struck, as he'd been before, by the contrast between the casinos and the world outside. The clear blue lake, the mountains, the pines might as well not even existed. Inside, the man-made lights glared down 24 hours a day. The smell of greed mingled with that of fear, with a whiff of sex thrown in for good measure as the casino girls in their abbreviated costumes served drinks while the dealers exhorted you to bet and the constant ringing of the slot machines made you feel that people, other people, were drowning in a cascade of money. It was time to leave.

He was on his way out when Zelda appeared. "Are you going?" she asked.

"Yes, I've had enough. How'd you do? Did you get attuned?"

"I did." She took a wad of cash from her purse and gave him a twenty dollar bill.

"Thanks."

"Thank you. My motel is right down the road. You're welcome to come."

Danny was tempted; she was an attractive girl. "No, I better not. I'm getting an early start tomorrow."

"All right, but be careful tomorrow. I have a feeling of danger. Don't do anything rash." Then she quickly turned and went back to the tables.

*   *   *

The next morning Danny was up early, had breakfast, then drove to the lake again. This time his thoughts were settled. There seemed no question as to what he must do. The freedom to do whatever he wanted that he'd sought and thought he'd found in San Francisco had gone to his head. He'd let himself get caught up in a whirl of drinking and partying. It was time to end it. He'd distance himself gradually from Gil Wexler and his gang and of course he wouldn't repeat what had happened with Ruth Baker. And he'd cut down on alcohol, maybe stop drinking altogether. No more going to a bar after work on Friday and continuing through the weekend.

Driving through the mountains on his way back to San Francisco, Danny found himself behind a slow-moving car. The driver was an old man with white hair. Danny could see him sitting bolt upright in the driver's seat. On the narrow twisting road it was impossible to pass him. Finally, they came to a straight stretch. Danny swung out and accelerated. Then he suddenly remembered Zelda White's warning. Be careful; don't do anything rash. He braked and pulled back. In that moment, a truck loomed up, speeding the other way. Danny could feel the wind as the truck rushed past. If he'd tried to pass—well, he didn't want to think about what might have happened.

Danny drove another 15 minutes until he found a place he could pull off the road. He took a deep breath and looked out at the tall pines around him. A squirrel came out from behind a shrub, seemed to stare directly at him, then raced away. He could hear birds chirping. After a while, his heart stopped pounding and he felt calm. Yes, he'd start a new kind of life when he got back to San Francisco. He felt very good when he thought this. He didn't know that an event would happen that would destroy all of his good intentions and send him off on another journey.

*   *   *

San Francisco: Being in Love

Danny had been asked to lunch, for the first time, by his boss Tommy Flowers. They were at a trendy (and expensive) restaurant in downtown San Francisco, frequented by ad agency, public relations and media types, with a few politicians thrown in. The luncheon invitation was by way of being a reward for Danny's working 60 hours the previous week on one of the surveys being done by Flowers' research firm.

Upon his return from Tahoe, filled with his good intentions, Danny had gradually withdrawn from the Berkeley gang although he still occasionally met Gil Wexler after work for a drink. Danny would order a ginger ale, which he'd nurse, while Greg would have his usual beers. From what Greg told him, Danny inferred that Greg and Ruth Baker were still going together and in fact were getting pretty serious. Danny felt a certain relief at this. That one night with Ruth that had caused him so much anguish hadn't had any real consequences.

Danny had also joined the Jewish Community Center, which had several four-wall handball courts. He'd had to adapt his game from playing one-wall but after awhile was playing pretty well and was in a group with some of the Center's better players. No money games but still competitive. So far his bursitis had not flared up again. Besides this, he'd thrown himself into his work, mostly surveys, which he found interesting. After three months, Tommy had given him a raise. He didn't mind working overtime.

"Have a drink," said Tommy, ordering one for himself.

"No thanks," said Danny.

"You don't drink and I know you don't smoke," said Tommy, as he lit a cigarette. "You're going to ruin the reputation of the firm. Should I ask you about girls?"

Danny did not have to think of an answer because at that moment a beautiful young woman, blonde, tanned, dressed in an immaculate white suit, entered the restaurant and stood for a moment looking around. Their attention, like everyone's in the restaurant, was focused on her, as if she stood in a spotlight.

Evidently seeing whomever was waiting for her, the young lady moved gracefully and purposefully through the crowded tables. As she passed them, Tommy said, "Hello, Julie." She stopped and said hello. Tommy knew everyone and everyone knew him.

"Allow me to introduce you to one of my new colleagues," said Tommy. "Danny Stein. He's from New York. Danny, Julie Landis. She's with Popper and Tuttle."

Danny stood up quickly, letting his napkin fall from his lap and knocking a fork off the table. Julie Landis was almost as tall as he was. She extended her hand and smiled, showing brilliant white teeth. Her grip was firm. Danny thought her eyes were gray, or were they green? After a long moment, he realized he was still gripping her hand and let it fall. She looked amused. "Welcome to San Francisco," she said.

"Thanks," said Danny. His voice sounded strange to himself, as if he'd run out of breath. He sat down as Tommy said, "I'll give you a call, Julie. Let's have lunch."

"Fine, Tommy." She smiled again and continued making her way through the tables.

"Smart girl," said Tommy. "And not bad-looking. She's assistant research director at P and T. Of course, they don't have much of a research department. We've done a couple of jobs for them in the last year, always an emergency."

"How old is she?"

"I don't know. In her late twenties, maybe. Why?"

That would make her only two or three years older than him. "Just curious."

The waiter came back with Tommy's drink and they ordered lunch. Tommy knew a good many stories and he told them well. Ordinarily, Danny listened with fascination. But this time he hardly heard what Tommy was saying. All thoughts of Ruth Baker, Sarah Cohen or Marilyn Gold had been wiped from his mind. He could only think about Julie Landis.

*   *   *

The next morning, as Danny walked to work, the sun shining, the sky blue, no fog, he thought he saw Julie Landis walking ahead of him on Montgomery Street. He hurried along but when he got closer saw that it was another tanned blonde young woman. There were quite a few in San Francisco. That weekend he was up early on Saturday, cleaned his apartment, did some shopping and wrote a letter to his parents back in New York. He also wrote his monthly checks, including the car payment for the used Volkswagon he'd bought. When he was done, he was pleased to see that his balance was a little higher than it had been the month before.

That night Danny went to a party he'd been told about it by one of the media salesmen he'd met at work. He'd decided it was time for him to get out and about. The apartment in which the party was being held was already filled with people when he arrived. Danny suspected that very few of them knew each other and that most had heard of the party second-hand as he had.

He looked around. He'd thought that Julie Landis might possibly be there (was that why he'd come?) but even as he looked he realized that it had been a far-fetched notion. The only person he recognized was Paul Marks, who did research in the local branch of one of the national ad agencies. Paul was in his early thirties, also from New York. He and Danny had met at meetings of the San Francisco Marketing Association. Paul always had a lot of information about the ad agency scene in San Francisco and sometimes it was even accurate.

"How're things at the firm?" asked Paul.

"Fine."

"Business not falling off?"

"Not that I know of. Have you heard anything?"

"Not really. But it's a pretty small place, you know. Maybe you should start looking around for some bigger outfit."

"I like it being small. I'm getting a lot of good experience. I met Julie Landis the other day, the assistant research director at P & T. Do you know her?"

"I've heard about her. Supposed to be quite a dish. I hear she has a thing going with the agency president, George Armstrong."

"Oh." They talked a little more. Danny talked to a few more people he knew. He made no attempt to meet any of the girls who were there by themselves. He drank only a couple of ginger ales and left early. Back in his apartment, he considered Paul's comment about Julie Landis and decided to discount it. He imagined calling Julie at her agency and asking her out but knew he'd never do it.

*   *   *

During the next two weeks, Danny worked normal hours at the firm. Tommy Flowers seemed to be out a great deal. Then on a Friday morning Tommy called him into his office and Julie Landis was sitting in the visitor's chair. She was wearing another suit, this time a dark green. Her short skirt showed off her legs and Danny couldn't help looking at them. "You remember Julie, don't you?" said Tommy. "P & T wants us to do a phone survey for them. A quickie. They need the results by the end of next week. I'd like you to do the number-crunching. It'll be more overtime."

Danny coughed to clear his throat. "That's okay," he said. "I'm just about caught up."

"Good." Tommy stood up from behind his desk and handed him a folder. "Take a look at this." He turned to Julie. "Are you ready for lunch?"

Julie stood up. "Do you have any questions?" Tommy asked Danny, who was still standing in the doorway, watching Julie.

"No," said Danny. He was evidently not going to be asked to join them for lunch. "I'll look this over right away."

*   *   *

The telephone survey was ostensibly to find out about people's shopping habits but its real purpose was to ask about a new household product of one of P & T's major clients, which was being test-marketed and had been on the shelves for three months. Danny quickly read through the survey plan and the brief questionnaire, asking if the product had been bought and, if so, how had people liked it. Respondents were encouraged to answer by the offer of a one-dollar off coupon.

The phoning started the next Monday and by Tuesday afternoon Danny was getting computer printouts of the results. He worked late every night, assembling figures into various tables. by sex and age, location, income, number of times shopping in a week, stores patronized. The client wanted a very detailed report.

Danny was still working on his tables around seven Thursday night. Everyone else in the office was gone. He heard a noise and, looking up, saw Julie Landis. "Hi," she said. "I thought I'd come over and see if you needed some help. Our client's been calling about the survey every day."

"Hi," he said. "If you don't mind doing some calculating. There's still a dozen or so tables to finish."

"I'm an old hand at calculating. How's it look so far?"

"Not bad. A pretty good market share for a new product and most people liked it. I've changed the geographical areas a little. The ones you had seemed too broad and gave some strange results."

She came over to his desk and stood next to him, looking at the tables. He could smell her perfume. Although she wore her usual suit, he was acutely aware of her breasts beneath her blouse and jacket. As always when he was near her, he felt out of breath and his throat seemed clogged up. "I see what you mean," she said. "That's much better. Can I use that desk over there?"

"Sure."

She briskly took off her jacket, sat down and got to work. Danny tried to focus on the figures before him, which appeared to be swimming around on the paper. "Be professional," he told himself. "Be professional."

They finished at ten o'clock. Danny showed her his report summary, everything boiled down to one page so that the client could see the survey findings at a glance. Julie read it quickly, then made a few penciled notes. "Just cosmetic," she told Danny. "I know the style they like. I think it'll go over well."

After Danny had put his draft on the secretary's table, to be typed first thing in the morning, they left the building. The street outside was deserted and the night air was cold; the famous San Francisco fog had come in. "I hope I can get a cab," said Julie.

"I'll drive you," Danny said quickly. "I knew I'd be working late tonight so I drove in."

She hesitated. "Are you sure you don't mind?"

"No. It's fine."

They went to the building's small parking lot, where Danny's Volkswagon was the only car left. She told him where she lived, a Pacific Heights address. When they arrived there, she said, "Come on up for a drink. We have to celebrate."

"Well, okay."

She turned on the lights as they entered and said, "Sit down and make yourself comfortable. I'll be right back." The living room was large and nicely furnished but somehow the apartment was not as impressive as Danny had thought it would be. He'd imagined a place high up in some tall building with a view of the city. He walked over to the window and looked out. There was no view, only other buildings with the fog swirling in between. Well, as he knew from his experience with Namm and Singer, ad agency researchers, even those with a title, didn't make a lot of money. That was reserved for copywriters and account executives.

When Julie came back, she opened a cabinet, which Danny saw contained a number of liquor bottles. "What will you have?" she asked.

"Whatever you're having."

"All right." She came over with a glass for him. Lifting her own, she said, "Here's to a happy client."

She'd taken off the suit jacket and also her shoes because she was now definitely shorter than Danny and somehow seemed less formidable. "Sit down," she said, and they sat at opposite ends of a long sofa. "So, tell me why you came to San Francisco."

Danny told her of going to college on a scholarship, majoring in English because he really didn't know what he wanted to do, then of his long search for a job because everyone seemed suspicious of an English major who didn't want to go into teaching. He recounted some of his adventures with Namm and Singer but didn't tell her of his dissatisfaction with the advertising business as she worked for an agency. He said he kept on hearing what a great city San Francisco was and so he'd decided to give it a try. He didn't tell her anything about Marilyn.

She told him she'd come to San Francisco four years ago, from Minnesota.

"Minnesota? I thought you were a California girl."

"No, not at all. My family are Swedes. That's where the blonde hair comes from. I think I came here to get out of the cold." Danny had almost finished his drink and as usual the unaccustomed alcohol had made him a little light-headed. Or was it the proximity to Julie? Somehow they had moved closer together on the sofa. He made a decision. This was probably going to be his one and only chance. He kissed her.

He waited for her to push him away. But she put her arms around him and pressed her lips against his. After a few minutes, she said, "Let's go to the bedroom."

*   *   *

Danny had returned to his apartment at about two AM, quickly undressed and fallen into his bed but when the alarm rang at 6:30 he was wide awake. After a quick breakfast, he walked to work. Last night's fog was gone and the sun was shining, sparkling off the windows as he strode along. Between buildings, he caught glimpses of the Bay, a bright blue. Once or twice he saw a blonde woman and thought she was Julie but he knew by now that it wouldn't be and he wondered if this would be happening the rest of his life. He knew that what he felt about Julie Landis was different from what he'd felt about Marilyn or Ruth Baker. He was in love. Or was it an infatuation? All he knew was that he couldn't stop thinking about her and that he imagined he saw her everywhere. All right, he was in love.

When he arrived at his building, he noticed for the first time its elaborate architecture, all the swirls and contours. As soon as he entered the office the secretary, who was already typing up his report on the telephone survey, called him over with a question and he was caught up in the business of the day.

Just before lunch he called the P & T agency and asked for Julie but was told she was in a meeting. He left a message but she didn't call back. He called again several times in the afternoon but each time was told she wasn't available. The last time he left another message, just his name and home phone number and asked that she call him. He stayed in all day Saturday in hopes that she might call but the phone, no matter how long he stared at it, never rang. On Sunday, he felt he had to get out and on an impulse he drove over the Golden Gate Bridge to Marin county. He went as far as Santa Rosa before he told himself this was foolish and turned around to go back.

He was about to go home from the office on Monday when Julie called. "Did you get my message?" he asked.

"Yes, but I was away all weekend. I wanted to tell you that our client was pleased with your report."

"That's good. When can I see you?"

"This is not a good time. I'm tied up with meetings all week and then I may have to go to Los Angeles."

"Will you call me when you get back?"

"I'll try. I have to go now. Good-bye."

*   *   *

Two weeks later Danny went to the annual meeting of the San Francisco Marketing Association. It was a large affair in the ballroom of a downtown hotel. He thought he saw Julie in the crowd and this time, when he made his way closer, it was her. She was talking to a tall white-haired man in an obviously expensive suit. "Hi, Julie," he said.

"Danny. How nice to see you. This is my boss, George Armstrong. Danny's the one who did that phone survey."

"Oh, yes. Very good work." Armstrong spoke with a faint British accent.

Another man came up to them and Danny was introduced to him but forgot his name immediately. Suddenly they seemed to be in the center of a swirling crowd and Julie was being swept away from him. "I'll call you next week, okay?" he called out. He couldn't quite hear what she replied but he thought she nodded her head, Yes.

*   *   *

When Danny finally talked to Julie the next week she again said she was busy but agreed to meet him on Friday for lunch. Danny considered all the places to eat and made reservations at a small restaurant which was not an ad agency hang-out and where he hoped they'd be able to talk.

But Thursday night he started feeling unwell. He couldn't believe it as he was never sick. He took some aspirin and went to bed early. The next morning he felt dizzy and could hardly stand up. It was clear he couldn't go anywhere that day. He called his office and then left a message for Julie that he was sick and wouldn't be able to make it.

All weekend he hoped that Julie would call, but she didn't. By Monday he was feeling better and went into work. He called her again and as usual she wasn't available. He left a message asking if they could have their lunch that week. On Wednesday night he was surprised when she called him at home. She was glad he was feeling better. "Why don't you take tomorrow off and we'll go for a ride?" she said.

"But they're expecting me in the office."

"Do you have anything that can't wait."

Actually, he didn't. In fact, things had been slow since the phone survey. "No, I guess not."

"I'll do the driving this time. Give me your address and I'll pick you up around ten."

*   *   *

She drove a little red sports car convertible with the top down. "Where are we going?" he asked.

"For a ride in the country. You'll see. And we're having a picnic. I have everything packed in a basket. It's in the trunk."

At the rate of speed she drove and with the car's top down, it was impossible to talk. She took the same route as he'd done when he'd gone on that aimless drive a few weeks before. She drove over the Golden Gate Bridge and then up toward Santa Rosa but then she turned off the main highway and went toward Sonoma. It was a fine day. The sun shone down on lush green hills. Every now and then they passed a herd of grazing cows. She turned down another road and they were off in the country with no one else in sight.

She drove a little ways along a dirt path, then stopped and jumped out of the car. "Here we are," she said. She handed him the picnic basket and took a blanket out of the trunk. She led him up a hill and spread the blanket out on the grass beneath a large tree on its crest. They could see other hills and a blue pond in the distance.

"This is a great place," Danny said.

"I found it driving around last year. Are you fully recovered?"

"I think so. But I called in this morning and told them I'd had a relapse and couldn't come in."

She opened the basket and spread out bread, cheese and fruits on the blanket. She also took out a bottle of wine and two wine glasses. "We used to go on picnics all the time in Minnesota," she said. "They don't seem to do that in California."

Julie was wearing a white tee-shirt with a light blue sweater over it, jeans and tennis shoes. She looked younger and, thought Danny, absolutely adorable. She continued to talk about her days in Minnesota. "My parents were shocked when I told then I was going to San Francisco. They couldn't believe I was going to that sinful city."

"My mother told me that if I left I needn't come back. She was disowning me."

"Poor parents," she said.

They ate and talked, then Danny took her in his arms and kissed her. He put a hand under her tee-shirt and felt for the clasp of her bra. "No," she said. "Not now. Just hold me."

They lay down on the blanket and looked up at the puffy white clouds. Every now and then, he kissed her lightly or caressed her hair or ran his hand over her breasts. But she wouldn't allow him anything more.

Eventually it became cooler and then cloudy. "We'd better be going," said Julie. They packed up and she drove him back to his apartment. "It was a nice day, wasn't it?" she said.

"Yes. Do you want to come up?"

"I'd better not. I have a dinner I have to go to tonight. An agency thing."

"When will I see you again?"

"Danny, I don't think we should. My life is, it's too involved."

"Oh. Can I call you every now or then?"

"Please don't. It would make it harder. Maybe the agency will need another survey and I'll see you again." She leaned over and kissed him. "I really have to go now."

In his dark apartment that night, Danny lie on his unmade bed, clasping his arms around his chest. He hadn't known it would hurt so much. When he'd had the flu, or whatever it was, he'd taken some pills and it had gone away. But there was nothing he could do to make this pain go away.

*   *   *

A few weeks later, Tommy Flowers gathered together his small staff and announced that, owing to various financial problems, the firm was being closed. Everyone would get severance pay and of course good recommendations.

When he looked back on it, Danny realized he should have suspected something. He remembered Paul Marks asking him at that party how the firm was doing and suggesting that he look for a job with a larger organization. Then there were all of Tommy's unexplained absences from the office. He should have known something was going on. But the only thing he'd been thinking about then was Julie Landis.

*   *   *

Danny had noticed that often when you thought about a person you met him soon after. He ran into Paul Marks on Montgomery Street after a discouraging interview with an employment agency that specialized in research jobs.

"Yeah," said Paul, after hearing about the interview. "A couple of agencies have cut back on research, a couple of the big companies, too. A lot of people are looking out there. Say, you know your friend Julie Landis. I heard she might marry her agency head, George Armstrong. I guess that's getting job security. Look, I have to run. Let's do lunch sometime."

"Sure." They both knew that this wouldn't happen.

Later on, Danny thought that this time was probably the low point in his life. After he left Paul Marks, he walked back to his apartment. He hadn't cleaned it in quite a while. As usual, dishes were in the sink, books and papers were scattered around. The few pieces of furniture were dusty. He thought about getting something to eat, then decided he wasn't hungry. He was tired though, very tired, as if he'd been in a 20-round fight or climbed up a steep hill. He sat in his one good chair and closed his eyes. Julie Landis came through the door and walked over to him. She bent over and kissed him. He could feel the feathery touch of her lips and smell her perfume. He opened his eyes. Julie was no longer there. He looked around. The dirty dishes in the sink and the papers were still there. It had become dark outside. He wondered how long he'd been asleep. He tried to clear his head. In the space of a month, he'd lost Julie Landis, not that he'd ever had her, he knew, and he'd lost his job. What had happened to his great plans when he'd left New York for San Francisco? Maybe he'd been wrong to leave what was after all his home to come out here. Look at where it had landed him. He stood up painfully. He'd better clean up the place.

*   *   *

San Francisco: Getting Married

It was a weekday afternoon. Danny was walking disconsolately along San Francisco's Fisherman's Wharf, having just been treated to lunch at the city's finest seafood restaurant. It was one of those bright, sunlit days when San Francisco seems magical, its light-colored hills appearing to float over the clear blue Bay, the venerable Golden Gate Bridge sparkling as if brand-new. Danny had just about made up his mind that he'd be leaving all this and returning to the grim reality of New York City.

The decision, which he'd been wrestling with over the last month, came down, as many things do, to a simple matter of economics; more specifically, having a job. He'd gotten the job with Tommy Flowers research firm so easily. Now he'd discovered how difficult it was to find work in a city to which thousands of talented young people flocked every month. The job openings of which he'd heard when working all seemed to have disappeared. Everyone was friendly enough when he called or dropped in, but nothing was available. His savings were dwindling and his unemployment insurance was running out.

There seemed only one thing left for him to do: return to New York. After all, the largest market research firms were headquartered there. His family and his old friends were there. Who knows, maybe his old girl friend, Marilyn Gold, who'd cried when he'd left for San Francisco, would still be there, waiting for him.

The only problem was that he'd left New York to get away from all that, the track he was supposed to follow: go to college, get a job, marry a nice Jewish girl (like Marilyn), then start a family, probably move to a little house out on Long Island when he could afford it. The track was clearly marked because this was exactly the way all of his old friends had gone. Well, maybe he was supposed to go that way, too. In ten or twenty years time, that escape to San Francisco, if he still remembered it, would seem like a little diversion, a minor blip in the course of his life.

Then had come the feeler from the food company which had its main office in San Francisco; they were considering hiring another research project manager and would he like to interview for the job? He had interviewed once, then again, then once again, his hopes going up and down, while the company tried to make up its mind over what it apparently viewed as a monumental personnel decision. On his part, he'd told himself that if he didn't get this job then he'd most likely go back to New York. The lunch he'd just come from had been the final installment in the food company drama; the marketing director himself, after telling Danny how impressed they were by him, had then said they'd decided to hold off hiring anyone for now.

Danny had by this time left the Wharf area and come to Hyde Street. He decided to go into the Beuna Vista, the bar that overlooks the Bay, for an Irish coffee, maybe a last one in San Francisco. As if conjured up by Danny's recent thoughts of him, there was Tommy Flowers at the bar, as dapper as ever in seersucker jacket, striped shirt and trademark red bowtie, looking as if his firm's bankruptcy had never happened.

"Hi, kid," said Tommy when he saw Danny. "Let me buy you a drink."

Danny thought, Why not? Tommy had cost him his job and most of his savings, he might as well have a drink at his expense. He ordered an Irish coffee. Tommy looked closely at Danny. "You didn't get the job, did you, kid?" he said. Danny didn't recall mentioning the food company to anybody, but then Tommy had always known everything that was going on.

"No, a nice lunch but no job."

"That's too bad. What are you going to do now?"

"Maybe go back to New York." And, in that moment, as he speaks the words, Danny knew he'd made his decision: he was going back.

*   *   *

The next morning Danny walked from his apartment to a nearby park. It was another sparkling day. The park was on a hill and from the bench on which he sat Danny could see the white sailboats fluttering like great birds on the Bay. Someone else sat down on the other end of the bench, a young man of about his age, blonde and tanned, looking like a California surfer. The young man commented on the view and they fell into conversation. Danny found himself telling about how he'd lost his job, the months of looking for work, and then his deciding to go back to New York.

The other young man listened sympathetically, then said, "Sounds like you've had a tough time," while he placed a tentative hand on Danny's thigh.

Danny immediately moved away, saying, "Hey, you've got the wrong idea." He stood up and began to walk away. He'd gone about ten steps when he heard a voice behind calling him.

"Hey, I'm sorry, okay," said the young man. "Look, I work in a State agency down at the Civic Center. I'm pretty sure they're looking for some research people. You don't sound as if you're that hot to go back to New York. I can give you the name of the guy to see. Why don't you check it out?"

Danny often wondered, especially after the onset of the AIDS epidemic, what had happened to the young man he'd met in that San Francisco park. What event or chance meeting had determined his life, or was it his death?

*   *   *

The Pacific Ocean looked calm and peaceful. Danny had driven out that morning and parked in the lot where the Cliff House was. In the past few months, since being unemployed, he'd driven out there several times. He'd always felt that looking out on the Pacific, seeing the waves coming in onto the beach in their unending succession made him feel better. If nothing else, it took his mind from the city that lay behind him, a city that, at the moment, seemed to have no use for him.

He walked to the seawall and looked out. As usual, a few men had their fishing poles planted in the sand. Danny had never seen anyone catch anything. Some people were walking their dogs along the edge of the ocean, the dogs running happily through the water. It was warm today and two or three families had spread blankets and taken out baskets of food. The kids ran into the water, which Danny knew was freezing, and shrieked with the cold.

The day after his encounter with the guy on the park bench Danny, as he'd been advised, had gone to the City Center where the big State Building was. He'd found the man whose name he'd been given and who was a clerk in Personnel, or Human Relations, as the State called it. Yes, they were looking for research analysts. Danny filled out an application form and attached his resume to it. The clerk, when he looked them over, seemed impressed. He told Danny he had good qualifications. Danny wondered if not too many people who'd worked in the private sector applied for a State job. Certainly, in all the time he'd been looking for work he hadn't considered it.

The clerk told Danny that, if hired, he'd start at the entry level, then he'd have to take a written exam in two or three months time and if he passed he'd move up to the journeyman level. He told Danny his papers would be processed and he'd get a call later in the week.

Danny waited anxiously the next few days. When the call came it was almost anti-climatic. The same clerk he'd seen told him there were several jobs open and he could come in on Monday, talk to the section chiefs and see which one he liked. Here he'd gone unemployed for months, thought Danny, and now he had his pick of jobs. Yes, life was funny.

Danny was to start work the next week. No more driving out to the ocean. Well, he could drive out on weekends, only then it would be crowded and he doubted that he would. He felt hungry, time for lunch. He took a last look at the ocean. He'd be entering a new world, working for the State. What would it be like? No matter what, he'd be able to stay in San Francisco and that was good.

*   *   *

Danny sat alone at a table for two in a restaurant on Polk Street in San Francisco. As he doggedly consumed a dinner which was large but not very good, he reflected that eating was probably the number one problem for a single male living by himself.

Cleaning his apartment was a pain, but that could be done only once a week, if that often, and his apartment was so small it didn't really require much. Besides, as nobody else ever came into his place, what did it matter? Taking his dirty clothes to the laundromat was also a pain, but that too was only once every week or, if he stretched it, two weeks.

But eating was something that had to be faced every day. Should he eat in or go out? Lately, he'd been trying to economize by cooking his own meals. But cooking for one was tedious and time-consuming, made even worse by having to clean up afterwards. He could always fall back on TV dinners, but he'd never felt these were real food, and they weren't that cheap, either.

When he was working in Tommy Flowers' research firm Danny had rarely even considered eating in, much less cooking for himself. Dinner meant going out to eat. But in those days he was making a good salary. Now, on his meager pay as a novice State employee, going to a good restaurant was a luxury he couldn't really afford. This was why, after getting home after a frustrating day in the office and feeling too tired to fend for himself, he'd gone to an inexpensive neighborhood place.

There was also the discomfort of eating out alone. In this restaurant, fortunately, a dozen or so other diners were men, sitting, like Danny, at small tables against the wall and trying to be inconspicuous. Danny looked around and saw one man, in his mid-thirties, recognizable in that his head seemed to be set directly upon his shoulders, whom he'd seen in the restaurant before, and whom he thought he'd seen working in the State building.

It was funny but there seemed to be an unusual number of odd-looking people working for the State. He'd noticed a woman who looked like a dwarf, a tall man who wore a beard which gave him a resemblance to Abraham Lincoln, and another man with an eye-patch giving him a piratical look. The State seemed to be a haven for people who wouldn't fit into a normal work setting, certainly not in the offices where he'd worked before. He smiled to himself when he remembered his chance meeting with someone in a park, the gay guy who'd tried to pick him up. It wasn't an unusual occurrence in San Francisco. But it was thanks to this guy that Danny had heard the State might be hiring research analysts. Well, he hadn't done too well in the private sector himself. Maybe the State would be a haven for him.

*   *   *

Danny walked the two blocks back from the restaurant to his apartment building on Octavia Street. It was August and so still light but already getting chilly, a typical San Francisco summer evening. He took the day's mail out of his box and opened the front door. As he entered, another tenant came in with him. She was young, no more than 21 or 22, and quite pretty. "Hi," she said to him.

"Hi." He'd never seen her before.

"Oh, look," she said. A small black and white cat had appeared in the hallway. "Is it yours?"

"No, it's not mine."

"It doesn't have a collar. I wonder if it's a stray who got in."

"Maybe."

She reached down to pet the cat but it darted around a corner. "Well, I'll see you," said the girl.

Danny walked up the three flights to his apartment. As he was spending most of his time there he was now trying to keep it neat and tidy. His refrigerator was filled, something that not long ago would have been unthinkable. He sat down and looked through his mail, which consisted of appeals for him to buy something, subscribe to something or donate to something. He remembered that he'd had a letter from his mother in New York two weeks ago which he hadn't answered. He'd do it on the weekend, after he'd swept and vacuumed.

He stood up, went into the kitchen and washed some dishes. After this, he got out one of his old statistics books and placed the armchair so that he could look out of the window. His apartment faced west and if he looked out at an angle he could get a glimpse of the Bay Bridge. The apartment had been advertised as having a view.

Danny opened the book. In two months, the State was giving an exam for the next level of research analyst, which would pay a few thousand more a year and he spent most of his evenings studying for it. Even a few thousand dollars more would do a lot for his standard of living. He'd also like to move on to another job.

The small unit Danny was in made surveys of the earnings and hours worked by employees in various industries. He'd chosen to work in it because of his experience in doing surveys. These had all been made with the idea of determining consumer likes and dislikes and ultimately selling products. It wasn't clear exactly what was done with the information produced by the State surveys, but evidently there was a State law which mandated that they be done. The next survey being planned was of drug store employees. In the past, questionnaires had been sent out to each and every drug store in the state. Danny had proposed surveying just a sample of drug stores and he'd spent most of that day trying to explain how this could be done to his unit chief and boss, Mr. Sprague.

Sprague's job title was Senior Research Analyst but Danny was sure that he knew next to nothing about actual research methods. He was also a typical State manager in that he was deathly afraid of trying anything new. Although Danny had come up with figures showing how much cheaper a sample would be, Sprague was opposed to it because that had never been done before.

Danny read for an hour or more before his mind started to wander. By this time it was dark and the lights of the cars streaming across the bridge were like a string of diamonds. As usually happened at night, his thoughts involuntarily drifted to Julie Landis. He closed the book and watched some mindless television for a while. This was usually how spent his evenings, having dinner in or occasionally, as tonight, eating out at some cheap restaurant, studying, television. He still played handball at the Jewish Community Center. On weekends he sometimes wandered around Golden Gate Park, observing that everyone except himself seemed to be a couple. Although he still thought of Julie Landis he was sure he'd gotten over her, pretty sure. It was time for bed. Before falling asleep, he thought about the girl he'd just met. He hadn't even asked her name. Well, she was awfully young. Danny would be 27 on his next birthday.

*   *   *

Danny and a co-worker, Hank Barrow, were in the Foster's cafeteria across the street from the State Building. Hank was the one who'd discovered that the cafeteria had a small bar which served surprisingly good drinks and they'd taken to dropping in on Fridays to celebrate the end of the workweek. Danny was no longer completely abstaining from alcohol. He' didn't think a drink or two once a week would do any harm It wasn't like his early days in San Francisco when going out for drinks on Friday was a prelude to an alcoholic weekend.

Hank was about Danny's age and had been hired at the same time. Like Danny, he'd had an interrupted career path. Danny thought that was why they'd become friends, or at least friendly. Hank had a master's degree and had taught at a small college before deciding he didn't like teaching. Danny suspected that Hank's parents were as upset about this decision as his had been about his deciding to move to San Francisco.

They exchanged the usual talk about their jobs. Hank asked Danny how he was getting along with Mr. Sprague.

"He's still against my sample proposal but he's going to let me write a memo about it. I have no idea where it'll go from there."

"If he lets Mr. Rose see it, maybe you'll have a chance."

Mr. Rose was the agency head and possibly the only manager, in Danny's opinion, who might know really something about statistics and research. At least, whenever he saw one of the new employees Mr. Rose always had a mathematical riddle to ask them.

"Maybe," said Danny, "but it's probably only his way of covering his ass if someone brings it up later. He can say that he seriously considered it."

"Well, you never know. They have to get up to date sometimes. Are you ready for the big exam?"

"I hope so."

"I bet you ace it. Do you want another drink?"

"No, I'd better be going."

"Hey, are you doing anything this weekend?"

Hank had asked that a few times and each time Danny had answered, untruthfully, that he was busy. But now he said, "No, not really."

"My sister is having a little party tomorrow night. Why don't you come?"

Danny was on the point of automatically refusing, but then he told himself, Why not? He didn't know how long it had been since he'd gone to any social event. He didn't have to be a complete hermit. "All right," he said.

Hank gave him the address and he wrote it down. "Thanks for asking me," he said.

"Sure. See you tomorrow night. Come around eight."

Danny's apartment building was a 20-minute walk from the Civic Center. He walked to work and back. Mickey, the stray cat he'd taken in, greeted him at the door. Mickey had become a big factor in Danny's life. It was nice to know that when he came home from work someone would be there. He'd taken to talking to Mickey and the cat always looked as if he was listening carefully. Danny patted Mickey's head, then opened a can of cat food for his dinner. He sat down in his armchair and looked through the day's newspaper. After a while,

Mickey jumped into his lap. Danny thought about the party to which he'd been invited. He knew Hank's sister was older than him and was a doctor at a hospital in Oakland. From remarks Hank had dropped, his parents were happy that she'd embarked on a successful career while Hank was still struggling to find his way.

The next day Danny spent an hour at the laundromat, then did some shopping at the local market. In the afternoon, he took a walk through his neighborhood. He had a TV dinner, read for a while and played with Mickey. "Well," he told the cat, "I'm going to leave you alone for a while tonight. I'm going to some kind of a party. I don't know what will happen, probably nothing, but it's a chance to go out. I'll tell you about it when I get back." At around eight, he left.

*   *   *

Hank greeted him at the door. About a dozen people were there, standing around with drinks and talking. Hank introduced him to his sister Anne. She was a woman in her mid-thirties, who looked a little like Hank, on the short side and stocky. She gave Danny a firm handshake and looked him over carefully. He wondered if she was curious about what kind of strange people her brother worked with at the mysterious State building or if, as a physician, she was examining him for signs of some infectious disease.

At any rate, after she'd asked him at least a dozen questions about their workplace she seemed satisfied and introduced him around. Most of the other people at the party also worked at the Oakland hospital. Danny wasn't very good at remembering names and faces but he did take notice of one girl, woman, he supposed. Her name was Ellen Carter and she was pleasant-looking, with long brown hair and greenish eyes behind round glasses.

He found out that she was an occupational therapist. After graduation, her first job had been at Bellevue in New York, working with mentally ill patients. She'd come out to California just six months ago and now she was doing the same thing in Oakland. She had a soft voice, a welcome contrast to the harsh accents he was used to in New York, and it turned out she was originally from the South, Atlanta, Georgia. Before their conversation could go any further one of the other guests, a tall fellow wearing a tweed jacket and khaki pants came over and joined them. Ellen introduced him as Dr. Something-or-Other. They seemed to know each other pretty well.

After listening to them talk for five or ten minutes about hospital matters he didn't at all understand, Danny excused himself and drifted around the room talking sporadically to one person and another. He ended up talking to Hank and after a while to Hank's sister Anne, who was very interested in the exam they had coming up. She wished that Hank was doing more studying for it. When Danny saw that it was ten o'clock he felt he could decently leave. He thanked Anne for letting him come and left. He was happy to get back to his apartment. "Well, Mickey," he said, "I went out and made it back. Nothing happened at the party. I met one girl I liked, but naturally she seemed to be with some other guy, a doctor. That always seems to happen to me. But I did get out for a while." He sat for a long time looking out his window, stroking Mickey in his lap, and thinking about Julie Landis.

The next week Hank surprised Danny by telling him that the girl he'd met at the party, Ellen Carter, had asked about him. He had her phone number, which his sister Anne had given him. "Why don't you give her a call?"

Danny recalled the intimate conversation Ellen had been having with her doctor friend. "Maybe," he said. He took the piece of paper with the phone number that Hank gave him and put it in his wallet, along with other forgotten papers he was holding onto for no particular reason.

* * *

The research analyst exam finally came and Danny thought he'd done fairly well. The exam was on a Saturday. That night he went to a movie by himself, thinking that he deserved a night out. He couldn't help noticing that almost all the other people in the theater were couples. On Sunday, he drove to Golden Gate Park, where again it was filled with couples. He spent most of the afternoon at the De Young Museum. That Monday night he remembered Ellen Carter's phone number in his wallet. He debated with himself for over an hour, arguing that by this time she would have forgotten him and in any case there was that doctor. "What do you think, Mickey" he asked. "Should I make a fool of myself?" He'd never entirely overcome his shyness, but he felt he'd somehow gotten a little tougher since Julie Landis and the debacle with Tommy Flowers' firm. "What the hell, what do I have to lose, right?" He steeled himself and dialed the number.

"You probably don't remember me," he said, thinking at once that this was a stupid way to begin. "Anyway, this is Danny Stein. We met at Anne Barrow's party a while ago. I work with Anne's brother Hank at the State."

"Oh, yes," she said. "I'd thought you'd forgotten me."

"No, it's just that I've been pretty busy. We had a promotional exam coming up and I've been studying for it. There were a lot of statistical questions and I was pretty rusty so I had to bone up. Anyway, the exam was last Saturday so it's over with now." What was he babbling about?

"Well, that must be a relief. How do you think you did?"

"Pretty good. I hope so anyway." They talked for a while, then Danny asked, "Are you doing anything next Saturday night?"

"I'm sorry, I do have plans."

"Oh. Well, maybe I can call you sometime again."

"I'm not busy Friday night."

"Okay, would you like to go out for a couple of drinks?"

"That would be fine."

She lived with two roommates on Clay Street, not far away. Danny said he'd pick her up at eight.

That Friday Danny and Hank had their usual after-work drink at Foster's. "So you're taking her out?" said Hank.

"Yeah. But she said she was busy on Saturday, so I don't know. She seemed to be very chummy with that doctor at the party."

"Hey, that was a long time ago. At least she remembered you, so you must have made some kind of impression. Give it your best shot."

Danny didn't know exactly what Hank meant by that but he said, "Sure."

The place Danny had chosen for their first date was the Laurel Lodge, a bar on California Street, which he remembered as being quiet and low-key. When they got there, he realized at once that it had changed in the last few years. There was a piano player and the music was loud rather than soft. The place was crowded and noisy. They found a small table next to a large one with a dozen or so young people who seemed pretty far gone, talking and laughing loudly.

When their drinks finally came, Danny said, "This used to be a much quieter place."

"That's all right. It's Friday night and everyone is blowing off steam. Look, we have popcorn. Good. I had to work late and didn't have much of a supper."

"They used to have little frankfurters here, too, by the fireplace. Let me see if they have any." Danny got up to look but found nothing. "Sorry," he said.

"I'll have to eat a lot of popcorn. So, when do you get your exam results?"

"I'm not sure, maybe not for a couple of months. That's how the State works. It's not exactly a streamlined process."

They talked some more about the exam and Danny hoped-for promotion. He told her something of his life before working for the State, the job with Tommy Flowers' research firm, the firm's unexpected closing and his search for another job. He didn't mention Julie Landis. She was curious about Tommy Flowers.

"What happened to him?" she asked.

"I heard he's gone to Sacramento. He's an aide to some assemblyman or state senator, something like that. That's about all I know. But I'm sure Tommy landed on his feet, whatever he's doing."

"Why don't you call him? Maybe he can help you with the State."

"I don't think so." The truth was that Danny had mixed feelings about Tommy. You couldn't dislike him but he felt Tommy had let down everyone in his firm. "I don't even know his phone number."

"You could probably find out."

"I'll wait for the exam results and then I'll see."

After they'd finished their drinks, Danny said, "Look, I have an idea. Speaking of Tommy, let's go to Tommy's Joint since you're hungry and get something to eat."

"The popcorn will be enough," said Ellen.

"No, let's go. I feel hungry, too, and Tommy's Joint will be better than putting up with those drunks at the next table."

Tommy's Joint on Geary Street is a San Francisco institution famous for it's good food, served Hofbrau style, its Irish coffee and its selection of beers from all over the world. It turned out that Ellen, although she'd heard of it, had never been there. They split a roast beef sandwich and had dark German beers to go with it. A group of four men between ages 40 and 50 sat next to them at the long table and, as often happened in San Francisco, one was from New York. They talked about New York and San Francisco and, when they learned that Ellen was from Atlanta, the South. After finishing the beers, Danny got Irish coffees. They stayed talking until around midnight, after the group of four had bought them a second round of Irish coffees.

When Danny brought Ellen to the door of her apartment, she told him she'd had a great time. He asked her about going out with him the next weekend, wondering if, like Marilyn back in New York, she would be busy every other weekend. But this time she wasn't busy on Saturday. He drove back to his apartment. He sat down and Mickey jumped onto his lap. He thought about the evening and realized he'd also had a great time. He also realized that Ellen, with her soft voice and slender body, reminded him of Marilyn. Maybe, Julie Landis aside, he was attracted to a certain type of girl. "What do you know, Mickey, I have a date next Saturday night. Maybe I won't end up being a hermit after all." Mickey meowed on hearing this.

*   *   *

The next week Danny attended a meeting on the drug store survey with Mr. Sprague. Mr. Rose chaired the meeting and several other agency managers were present. After a little discussion, one of the other managers, Danny thought he had something to do with finance, said that the survey budget was awfully high and couldn't they find some way to cut it. Mr. Sprague, after some hesitation, said they might be able to cut costs by doing a sample instead of, as in the past, surveying every drug store. Mr. Rose said that sounded interesting. Mr. Sprague said he could have a memo to him by the end of the week. After the meeting, he told Danny to re-write his memo and provide a detailed budget for Mr. Rose.

*   *   *

That Saturday was warm and sunny although it was already early October. Danny picked up Ellen in the afternoon and drove her over the Golden Gate Bridge to Sam's Anchor Cafe in Tiburon. As with Tommy's Joint, she'd heard of Sam's but hadn't been there. Sam's as usual was crowded but they managed to find two wooden chairs by a wooden keg that served as a table. Sam's, unlike the Laurel Lodge, was pretty much as Danny remembered it from the time he'd gone there with the Berkeley gang . . . People sat back in the wooden chairs taking in the sun while gazing at the view of San Francisco across the Bay.

He ordered two Samburgers and two beers. While they ate, noisy gulls swooped around, looking to grab food off someone's table. This was also as Danny remembered. "Careful," he told Ellen. "Hang onto your food."

He told Ellen about the meeting and the latest development about the drug survey. They were waiting to hear from Mr. Rose. She told him about her week at the hospital. Taking this as his cue, Danny asked about the doctor she'd talked to at Anne's party. "I did go out with him a few times," she said. "But he's like all doctors. He thinks he's God." When Danny brought her back that evening he kissed her and she responded, holding him close to her. She asked him to come over for dinner the next week.

*   *   *

Work had become more interesting, and much busier, since Mr. Rose had approved using a sample for the drug store survey, a cost-saving idea which Mr. Sprague duly took credit for as his own. But Danny didn't mind, or not too much. He spent his workdays developing what's known as a stratified sample, where drug stores were separated by employee size and a sample of each size range was selected. Of the many small-sized stores, only a few needed to be sampled and all of the very large stores were to be surveyed.

Danny had started seeing Ellen two or three times a week. He learned that her father was a lawyer who'd retired early because of severe arthritis. She had a younger brother who was still in college. Her family had lived in Georgia for three generations. She was the "wild" one who couldn't wait to leave home and see different parts of the world. While working at Bellevue she'd saved enough money to go to Europe for a year, then she'd worked a year in Vancouver before coming down to San Francisco. But Danny had the impression that she'd had her fill of travel and wanted now to get married and with marriage would come a family.

By now, Ellen had been to Danny's apartment and had met Mickey, who liked her, choosing to climb into her lap rather than Danny's whenever she was there. Then one Friday evening, after he'd stopped thinking about it, the exam result came in the mail. Danny had finished second statewide. He immediately called Ellen with the news.

"That's wonderful," she said. "Does this mean you'll get a promotion?"

"No, it just means that whatever job at that level comes open I'll be interviewed for it."

"But what about the job you're in now. Can't they just give you a promotion?"

"The State doesn't work like that. I'll ask first thing Monday, but Sprague has already just about told me that it won't happen." Danny didn't tell Ellen that the best chance for a promotion would be in Sacramento, the state capital, where almost all of the state agencies had their headquarters.

"That doesn't matter. I'm sure something will come up soon. We should celebrate."

"Well, the exam was the good news. The bad news is that my car's in the shop. The guy said I'll probably need a valve job."

"Is that very bad?"

"Yeah, a couple of hundred dollars."

"Oh, that is bad. But look, let's still celebrate. I'll buy some food and Marge can drive me over to your place."

"You don't have to."

"I want to. Besides, I haven't seen Mickey for a while."

When Ellen got there, she brought a bagful of groceries, which included a steak, a package of frozen French fried potatoes and a bottle of wine, which she unloaded onto the kitchen table. She also had another small plastic bag.

"What's in that?" asked Danny.

"You'll see later."

They finished dinner, which Danny told Ellen was great, then sat on the sofa-bed. Ellen pressed close to him and Danny kissed her. After a while, Danny, remembering Marilyn, said, "It's getting late. Do you want me to walk you home?"

"That won't be necessary." She got up and opened the plastic bag. It contained a short nightgown, a make-up case and a toothbrush.

"I don't know what Mickey will think," said Danny.

But when they opened the sofa-bed and got in it, Mickey curled up placidly in the armchair and went to sleep.

* * *

A few weeks later, Danny was walking through the Civic Center on his way back to the office after lunch when he heard his name called. It was a tall, curley-haired fellow in a bulky coat, who said, "I thought that was you. Remember me? Pete Mancuso. You did a couple of research projects for us."

Danny remembered. Pete was in the marketing department of a large paper products company on Montgomery Street. "Yeah, sure. What are you doing in this part of town?"

"I had a lunch meeting. I haven't seen you around for a long time. What have you been doing?"

Danny gave him a quick summary. He thought that Pete smirked when he heard that Danny was now working for the State.

"So you're feeding at the public trough, huh?"

"That's it."

"Say, didn't you used to know Julie Landis?"

At the mention of her name, Danny felt a shiver go through him. "Yeah, a little?"

"I thought so. She married her boss at the agency, you know, what was his name, Armstrong or something."

"Yeah, I think I heard about that."

"The word is now that they're splitting. It didn't last very long."

"Do you know what she's doing now?"

"I think she's with another agency, marketing director or something. I also hear she might be going to Los Angeles. She'll get to the top, no matter what."

"Yeah, I'm sure she will."

"Well," said Pete, "I have to run. Another meeting this afternoon. You know how it is. Hey, give me a call and we'll do lunch."

"Right," said Danny. He knew the chances of this were less than Sprague's offering him a promotion. He returned to his office and spent the rest of the day with his sample design.

*   *   *

Ellen was going home to Atlanta for the holidays but the agency's Christmas party was held early, around mid-December, so she was able to go to it. Danny was surprised that the party was held in one of the city's better restaurants. Everyone was dressed up in his or her best. Mr. Rose wore a blazer and one of his natty bowties. Even Mr. Sprague wore a suit which was less crumpled than usual.

During dinner, which was excellent, Mr. Rose made the round of tables. When he came to theirs, Danny introduced Ellen to him. "Why haven't you brought this lovely young lady around before?" demanded Mr. Rose, then without waiting for a response, he said to Ellen, "I don't know how much longer Danny is going to be with us. I wish we could promote him here, he's saved us a lot of money on a survey we're doing. But our hands our tied."

Mr. Rose asked Ellen some questions about herself, where she was from, how she liked San Francisco, then he passed on to another table. "I think he knows it's you and not Mr. Sprague that came up with that sampling idea," Ellen said to Danny.

"Mr. Rose usually knows what's going on in the agency."

"It's too bad he can't give you a promotion here."

"Yeah." Danny was on the point of telling Ellen that getting a promotion would most likely mean going to Sacramento, but he decided this wasn't the right time. He'd bring up that subject when she got back from her holiday vacation.

"Well, I'm sure something will come up."

*   *   *

Something did come up, much sooner than Danny had expected. Two days before Christmas, he got a call from a DeWitt Bender of the State's giant Health Department in Sacramento. The department had an opening for a mid-level research analyst. So during the week between Christmas and New Year's Danny found himself driving in the rain to Sacramento. After being passed around among three secretaries, Danny, holding his wet raincoat and a dripping umbrella, was ushered into Bender's office.

"Sorry to make you drive up on such a day," said Bender, standing up behind a large desk to shake Danny's hand. "One of our analysts left quite suddenly and we have to fill the position as soon as we can." He told the secretary to take Danny's wet things and asked him if he'd like some coffee?

Danny would have but said, "No thanks," as he didn't want to be juggling a cup and saucer while answering questions. Bender looked to be at least in his fifties. He was a gaunt man with furrowed cheeks and a shock of white hair. He sat slumped in his chair looking unbearably weary, as if he'd seen all the inane things that could happen in a State agency and nothing would surprise him any more. He was the assistant research director for the department.

Bender had Danny's resume in front of him and asked about his previous experience. When Danny described his work with Tommy Flowers, he said, "There's a consultant of that name working for the Legislature, I think."

"That's the same one."

"I see. Well, tell me about your present work."

Danny gave a summary of the drug store survey. Bender seemed impressed with the sample design as well as with the questionnaire he'd developed. Then Bender said, "We're trying to set up a computerized information system for one of our programs. Do you know" and he mentioned a computer language then widely used.

Without answering the question immediately, Danny quickly detailed all of the computer experience he'd had, which primarily had to do with tabulating survey questionnaires. He tried to sound as knowledgeable as possible, then concluded by saying, "I'm sure I could learn a computer language if I had to."

Bender said nothing to this, just slumped a little further down in his chair. They talked a little more and Bender asked if he could contact Danny's supervisor. Danny said that was no problem, then added that he could also call his agency chief, Mr. Rose. Bender said that he knew Rose from way back; he was quite a character. Danny agreed. Bender concluded by telling Danny they had two more candidates to interview and that he'd try to get back to him as soon as possible. He stood up and extended his hand, indicating that the interview was over. Danny gathered up his coat and umbrella and left the building. He told himself that he'd have to find out about learning the basic computer languages if that's what it took. At least it had stopped raining. He got into his car and drove back to San Francisco. He wondered if he should call Ellen about the interview and decided not to. There was no point to it unless he actually got an offer.

*   *   *

It was New Year's Eve. Danny was again at the apartment of Hank Barrow's sister Anne, who was giving a small and very sedate party. Ellen had called him earlier in the day and told him she wished she was there with him. Danny said he wished she was, too. Hank came over to where he was standing by himself. "Well, did you hear about the job yet?"

"No, nothing."

"You'll probably get a call next week. There's no question you'll get it."

"I don't know. I didn't know anything about actually writing computer programs."

"How many State research analysts do? Don't worry, the job is yours. So, what are you going to do about Ellen?"

"What do you mean?"

"Well, if you're going to Sacramento, you'll obviously have to take her with you. Have you popped the question yet?"

"You mean ask her to marry me?"

"Sure. She'll have to make an honest man of you."

"I hadn't really thought about it," Danny lied.

"Come on, you can't expect her to wait around for you while you're way up there in the boondocks."

"Actually, there's no reason why we can't see each other on the weekends. It's only a two-hour drive. I timed it."

Anne suddenly materialized beside them, a frown on her face. "You mean you'd go up to Sacramento just like that. You'd be a fool to leave her behind. Ellen's a wonderful girl. If you don't marry her, you deserve to lose her."

"Maybe she doesn't want to go to Sacramento," objected Danny. "She has a good job here."

"There are hospitals in Sacramento."

"Well, I may not even get the job."

"That's fudging it," said Anne firmly.

Before Danny could think of a reply to this true statement, someone said, "It's almost midnight." The TV was on, and thanks to tape delay, they watched the ball coming down in Times Square. It was snowing there. Everyone sang Auld Lang Syne, then turned to the nearest person and kissed. Anne was the nearest woman to Danny, but he didn't think this was the time to kiss her. He sipped his champagne, then at the earliest opportunity went back to his apartment and wished Mickey a Happy New Year.

*   *   *

Danny's parents called him on New Year's Day. He told them about the interview in Sacramento. He'd casually mentioned in one of his letters that he'd been seeing a girl named Ellen, just "seeing" as anything more than that would have his mother making wedding plans, and they asked him about her. He said that she was visiting her parents for the holidays. They said she sounded like a nice girl to be doing that. Danny agreed that she was a nice girl. "So are you getting serious?" demanded his mother. "You're not getting any younger, you know."

Danny said he'd see what happened when he knew for sure about the job. He changed the subject by asking about what they'd done on New Year's eve and if it was still snowing, then hung up as soon as he could.

The job offer came during the first week of January, brought to Danny by Mr. Rose himself. Mr. Sprague objected that they were in the middle of the drug survey and he couldn't afford to lose Danny. Mr. Rose told him not to worry, they had a replacement already lined up, a UC Berkeley graduate with a degree in statistics.

Bender called soon after to make it official and Danny accepted. At lunchtime, he told Hank, who asked him if he'd told Ellen yet. Danny said, "No, I'll call her tonight." Hank looked pointedly at him but said nothing. In the afternoon, on an impulse Danny decided to call Tommy Flowers. He called the information number for the state legislature and eventually was put through to a secretary, who told him Mr. Flowers was busy and he'd have to leave a message. At that point, Tommy's familiar drawling voice came on and said, "That's okay, Miss Flynn. I'll take this call. Danny, it's been a long time. How are you?"

Danny told him he'd gotten a job with the State, and would be coming up to Sacramento soon. Tommy said, "Yeah, I know. Old Bender gave me a call and asked about you. I told him you were a decent enough researcher."

"Thanks."

"Yeah. I also told him you could learn any computer language in no time flat."

"I hope you're right."

"Don't worry, you'll be okay. Call me when you get here and I'll buy you lunch."

"Sure. I'll see you." Danny hung up. He thought he'd always have mixed feelings about Tommy but he felt better for making the call.

*   *   *

That night, as he'd told Hank he would, Danny called Ellen to tell her about the job offer. She said she was thrilled that he'd be getting a promotion, then stopped, clearly waiting for Danny to say more. Danny had talked to some people in the office who'd once lived in Sacramento and he relayed to Ellen what they'd told him, that Sacramento was hot in the summer and foggy in the winter, but that housing cost much less than in San Francisco and of course, for a State employee, that was where the jobs were. Ellen didn't say much in reply, but when Danny said he was going up there that weekend to try finding an apartment she offered to go with him and help him look.

The next day Danny received a phone call in his office. "Hello, Danny." He hadn't heard Julie Landis's voice in over two years but recognized it instantly.

"How did you know I was working here?" he asked.

"I have my spies. It's too bad you had to take a job with the State." Danny was about to tell her of his impending promotion when he transferred to Sacramento, but she went on. "We have a research job here that I think would be perfect for you."

Danny's world suddenly seemed to turn upside down. "You have?"

"We have to fill it right away. Can you stop by my office at, say, six o-clock? Almost everyone else will be gone by then and we can talk."

Danny was off at five. "Yes, he said. "I can be there." After all this time, he would be seeing Julie Landis again.

*   *   *

Julie's agency, Danny could see, was a large one, located in one of the new buildings on Montgomery Street. A pretty receptionist greeted him and said that Ms Landis was expecting him. When he entered, Julie stood up, walked around her desk and shook his hand. He was reminded of their first meeting, in a restaurant where Tommy Flowers had taken him to lunch and when he'd instantly fallen in love with her.

"You're looking well for a bureaucrat," she said.

"Just a humble civil servant," said Danny. "You're looking well, too." She was, he thought. When he'd first met her he'd thought she was the quintessential California girl and he still did even though he'd since learned she was from Minnesota. She was as beautiful as ever, even though he could now see tiny lines around her eyes and she looked somewhat tired.

Instead of going back behind her desk, Julie sat down in an armchair and motioned Danny to one next to it. "Let me tell you about the job I had in mind," she began.

Danny listened but barely heard what Julie was saying. He was thinking that with this job he'd be back where he was when Tommy Flowers' firm went under. He'd be with one of the top agencies in town and he could stay in San Francisco, the lovely city by the Bay. He could forget about moving to Sacramento in the hot, dusty valley. He came to when Julie finished speaking. "Well, how does it sound to you?" she asked.

"It sounds good."

"And of course we'll be able to see each other." She leaned forward and put a hand on his knee.

* * *

Another decision time, thought Danny. This time he didn't drive to the ocean. For one thing, the weather was bad, cold and rainy. For another thing, he thought he was a little tougher than he'd been and knew his own mind better. Working for the State had been interesting. In a way, it had been like the Army. The State had its own system of ranks as had the Army, only instead of officers, noncoms and enlisted men there were job levels—entr6y-level, journeymen, associate, senior and then the upper-level managers. As with the Army, the different ranks rarely mingled with one another. He supposed he was an enlisted man and when he moved to his new job he'd be a noncom. The State was rigid and most managers, like Mr. Sprague, were made uneasy by change.

No, it wasn't the ideal place to work, but it did have his compensations. Your job was secure. By taking and passing exams you could rise through the ranks. The State would not suddenly go out of business. You could plan ahead. What would it be like working in Julie Landis's ad agency? What would happen if he didn't jump when an account exec called? Or when a client threatened to leave? Then there was the matter of staying in San Francisco. The city was fine when he was a young man still trying to find his way. But it was hard to imagine raising a family there. For one thing, houses were prohibitively expensive. Did he want to live in an apartment all of his life, even one with a view. And the city had gotten crowded. Traffic was terrible; it was hard to park anywhere. Of course, he knew these were side issues. The real decision was Ellen or another try at Julie Landis.

* * *

They'd driven to Sacramento in the morning. Unlike Danny's previous visit there, it was sunny and warm, even in February. The landlady, Mrs. Fish, was a blowsy heavily-made up woman of about 60 who waved a cigarette about while showing them the apartment. From the way she beamed at them, it was clear she thought Danny and Ellen were married. "How soon will you be moving in?" she asked.

"Uh, I'll be moving in," said Danny. "Ellen is just helping me look."

"Oh," said Mrs. Fish, her smile vanishing. "Well, I'll leave you two here to look around. I have to feed my cats."

"That reminds me," said Danny. "I have a cat. Is that okay?"

"Mmmm. Normally, I don't allow pets. I'll have to think about it."

When Mrs. Fish left, they sat down on the two chairs in the small living room. "It's not much, is it?" said Danny.

"It can be fixed up."

"At least it is a one-bedroom. You know, I bet the two of us can live here as well as one."

"What do you mean?"

"Well, what I mean is, I'd like you to come up to Sacramento and live with me. If you can give up your job. After we get married, of course."

"Danny, is that supposed to be a proposal?"

"A proposal. Yes, it is. Wait a minute." He stood up, then knelt beside Ellen's chair. "Ellen Carter, will you be my wife?"

"Danny Stein, I will." He kissed her. "I never thought you'd come out with it," she said.

"I had to. I know Mickey couldn't live without you."

"Mickey? What about you?"

"And me."

When Mrs. Fish came back, Danny told her that Ellen would be moving in with him after all; they were getting married. Mrs. Fish said there'd be no problem with their having a cat.

*   *   *

There was no bachelor party and the wedding itself would be small, in the Unitarian church on Geary Street. Only Hank and his sister Anne would be there. The idea was that they'd go back East sometime in the spring and visit New York so that Ellen could meet his parents and the rest of his family, then they'd go to Atlanta and he'd meet Ellen's parents and her family. On the night before the wedding, Danny took Hank to dinner at his neighborhood restaurant. "The food's not very good here, you know," said Hank.

"I know, but it's cheap. In a way, I'll miss it. I wonder if I'll ever eat at a place like this again." He looked around. The same single men, including the man with no neck who actually did work at a State agency, were sitting at the little tables along the wall. Well, he'd no longer be one of them.

"You won't be missing much," said Hank. "So you start work next Monday?"

"Yeah, Ellen, too. It was nice of Anne to call that Sacramento hospital about a job for her."

"I'll tell you something, I think she called over a month ago. I remember you telling me at that New Year's Eve party that you hadn't even thought of getting married. Actually, you never had a chance."

"I guess not."

"Think you'll miss San Francisco?"

"A little, but it's time I moved on. Once we get settled, we'll start looking for a house."

"And then come the kids."

"One step at a time." Yes, he'd miss San Francisco. An image of Julie Landis flashed across his mind. That part of his life was over. He was getting married.

*   *   *

Epilogue: Back in New York

"She's beautiful," said Danny's Aunt Anna.

"How did you get a girl like that?" asked his Aunt Rose. "So slender, like a model."

The entire Stein family was jammed into his parents' Bronx apartment and it was clear that everyone loved Ellen. Any thought that there might be a problem because she wasn't the Jewish girl they'd all expected him to marry had vanished. Danny's mother had immediately hugged Ellen and proclaimed her one of the family. She was probably relieved, thought Danny, that someone had actually married her wayward son. His father gazed fondly on Ellen as she went around the room, meeting everyone. Danny's mother had gone all out in her welcoming party. A table was loaded with cold cuts, cheese, herring, lox and breads. The air was filled with the aromas of New York foods. Everyone congratulated Danny. He wondered how it would be when they went to meet Ellen's family in Atlanta. How would they receive a Yankee from the Bronx, and a Jewish Yankee at that?

He made his way over to his cousin Ben and congratulated him on his marriage and his impending child. Ben's wife was noticeably pregnant. After a few remarks Danny asked, casually, he thought, if Ben knew what had happened to Marilyn Gold. Ben replied that he thought she was still teaching and he was pretty sure she was married. So, thought Danny, she hadn't pined away after he'd gone to California. He wasn't exactly sure how he felt about this. "I've heard you bought a house," said Ben.

"Yes," said Danny. "We closed just before we left."

Ben asked how much they'd paid and Danny told him. "You're lucky. Houses here cost twice as much. I don't know when we'll be able to afford one. You're lucky you decided to move to California?"

Lucky? Maybe, thought Danny. Certainly getting married and buying a house hadn't been on his mind when he'd made the move.

In bed with Ellen in his old room that night Danny felt tired out and stuffed with food. "You made a hit with my family," Danny told Ellen.

"Your mother said she thought you'd never get married."

"My mother said she'd disown me if I went to California."

"Then I guess she's changed her mind."

*   *   *

"No pastrami on rye in California?" said Zee.

"Not like this," said Danny.

They were having lunch in the old delicatessen they'd always gone to when they worked at Namm and Singer. Ellen had gone on a shopping expedition with Danny's mother. Danny and Zee were catching up. Zee had moved on to another agency, a larger and more stable one, where he'd become an assistant account executive. Danny thought that with his natural optimism and outgoing nature Zee would be a good account exec. Danny had asked if he was terrorizing lowly research analysts. Sure, Zee had said, they'd better jump when I call, or else.

"Is Jack Grossman still at Namm and Singer?"

"Still there and still worrying and the agency is still shaky."

"How about Henry Fox?"

"Would you believe it, he's gone into his father's clothing business. Says advertising is too cutthroat for him"

"That's surprising. Uh, what about Sarah Cohen."

"Even more surprising. She's married and has two kids."

"What?"

"Yeah, her husband is some rich guy, a former client."

"Wow!"

"So, how about you? Married, a homeowner. You seem to be doing okay?"

"Yeah, I think so."

"How do you like being a bureaucrat?"

"Well, it's not the greatest but I'm doing surveys, which I like, and the State is a lot more stable than an ad agency."

"Ah, job security. What all of us admen want and will never have."

"But all that glamour. So, do you have a girl friend?"

"No, still looking, but I'm having lots of fun."

Lots of fun. Danny wondered if he'd be having lots of fun if he's remained unmarried. Probably not. He didn't recall having a lot of fun before being married.

After finishing lunch and leaving Zee at the entrance to his glossy office building, Danny, as he'd known he would, walked up Madison Avenue to Central Park. As luck would have it, that particular spring day showed New York at its best. It was warm but mild and in the park a slight breeze felt good. The trees in the park were all leafed out, the sky was a pale blue. The men striding by looked prosperous, no job-seekers among them, and the women all seemed young and beautiful. Even the air smelled fresh, despite the exhaust of cars and buses. He remembered the walk to the park he'd made just after getting, finally, a job, the one at Namm and Singer.

Then he suddenly remembered Stanko, whose false letter of recommendation, had helped him get the job. He hadn't thought of Stanko in years. He vaguely recalled Stanko having said something about getting a Wall Street job. Back then, Danny hadn't known anything about stock markets, bond markets, mutual funds, all of that financial stuff. He really wasn't out to make money, just get a job so he could be independent. Now he thought about money a lot. He and a friend from his office walked over to a brokerage firm a couple of times a week. His friend urged him to get into a mutual fund. Maybe he would, after he and Ellen got settled in their house. Well, he wouldn't be surprised if Stanko had made a lot of money, that is, if he hadn't been caught doing something illegal and was in jail.

Thinking of Stanko led him to thinking of his old mentor back at Seventh Army Headquarters in Germany, the Colonel. He was sure the Colonel would have participated in some way in the Vietnam War. He wondered what the Colonel had thought of it. He recalled some of the Colonel's maxims: know the terrain, weigh your options, always have a way out. He wouldn't have been to happy with the way we'd conducted the war, Danny thought. What would he have made of Danny's return to civilian life? He probably wouldn't have approved of all the zigs and zags Danny had made. But if you couldn't plan for a war, too many things out of your control, you certainly couldn't plan for your life, where, it seemed, even more things were out of your control . . . Well, at any rate, he had a job and he had a girl, Ellen, his wife. He felt that one phase of his life, maybe phase one, was over; the next phase, with his marriage and then buying a house, was starting.

Danny sat down on a bench just outside of the zoo. He thought about the house and hoped it would turn out okay. He knew Ellen wanted a family. He did, too. That was one reason he was happy they'd moved to Sacramento. It might be a cow town when compared to San Francisco and certainly to New York. But it was hard to imagine having a family in San Francisco and impossible to imagine having one in New York. He remembered the day the troop ship had pulled into New York, the anticipation and anxiety he felt about embarking on his post-Army life. He felt pretty much the same way about the life he'd be entering when they returned, a house in the suburbs, then the kids. He stood up and started to walk to the zoo. He saw one of those food carts New York has and, as he'd done before, stopped to buy himself a salted pretzel.

THE SHORT STORIES

FOREWORD

As I did with my previous longer piece, I've added some short stories, published in online magazines during the past year and a half or so, to make up this book. The first three stories are a series about a "retired knight" in the time after King Arthur's reign in Britain when anarchy more or less took over the country. My thought was to use these stories to comment on the chaotic times we're undergoing at present. To hold the series together, I sent the knight on a journey to Camelot. In each story, he had some adventure on the way. I'm not sure at this point why he was going to Camelot and I see I stopped after three stories. Whether or not I resume the series remains to be seen.

The next two stories are also part of what might become a series, about people who are being profiled as "Residents of the Month" in the monthly publication of their retirement community. This is in fact what's being done in the paper I write for, the Sun Senior News, which goes to two retirement communities, Sun City Roseville (where I live) and Sun City Lincoln Hills. I thought this would be a good way of writing about interesting or unusual characters. At this date I've written just two "resident" stories, but I hope to do more as time goes by. By the way, in one of these stories, the resident of the month looks back regretfully at his earlier life and wishes he'd done things differently.

The next three stories revolve around a protagonist I've named Paul Lerner, who lives in a northern California retirement community suspiciously similar to Sun City Roseville. I've done a number of Paul Lerner stories, which I think of as "old guy" pieces. They deal with things that senior citizens (like myself) have to contend with or issues that arise in a retirement community. The rest of the stories are varied, some "speculative," such as "The Girl (?) Next Door," "Rajah," and "The Magic Racket."

A question usually asked writers is how do they come up with ideas for their stories. As it happens, no one has ever asked me this question. Possibly, people who know me and might have asked think my stories just appear out of thin air. Since, as I've mentioned earlier in this book, I've had over 250 short stories published in online magazines, I must have some method or methods of unearthing story ideas. So, even though no one might be interested, I want to write something about this.

The first short stories I wrote were almost all based on experiences I had in my own life. The first book I had out, which I called "Short Stories, Volume I," had sections on

"Growing Up in the Bronx," "Army Stories," "New York Stories," "San Francisco Stories" and "Sacramento Stories." Other stories have come in a variety of ways. One story, "The Promotion," started writing itself in my mind while I was in bed one night. A few stories have originated in dreams, the most recent being "The Drink." As I was walking from the bedroom to the kitchen one night I "saw" a boy next to a large tiger; this became the story "Rajah." In general, I'd say that for some reason things that are on my mind present themselves as stories, just as, say, they might present themselves to someone else as a mathematical equation.

In the past few years my stories have appeared primarily in three online magazines so I want to take this opportunity to thank their editors: Sam North of Hackwriters and Dave of Winamop, both English, and Dianne Kochenberg, Clever Magazine, San Jose, California. I also want to thank Julie Larson, publisher of Storystar, who not only prints my stories but also says nice things about me and my writing on Facebook. A good thing about Storystar is that it shows the number of views a story gets so I do know that a fair number of people have read them, which is satisfying as any writer likes to be read.

All of the stories following, whatever their origins, are fictional.

Roseville, California

February 2013

The Retired Knight
(Winamop)

The two rough-looking young men had suddenly appeared as 10-yeqr old Jack and his older sister Mary were on the way back to their farm from the market.

"Well, what have we here?" said the larger of the two.

"A likely-looking wench, Sir Charles," replied the other.

"I'm sure our lord would like to make her acquaintance, Sir Ronald"

This had become a common occurrence as the kingdom had descended into lawlessness after the death of King Arthur. The young people especially had thrown off all restraints, declaring that anyone over 30 couldn't be trusted and that now they were claiming their rights and could do anything they wanted. It was a turbulent time, in many ways similar to our own.

"I don't believe you're knights," said Mary, who was a plucky girl. "You're common hooligans. Now let us pass."

In response the one called Ronald grabbed Mary's arm. "Leave her alone," Jack shouted. He tried to get at Ronald but the other one, Charles, pushed him to the ground.

"Is there a problem here?" Another person had appeared, a knight in black armor seated on a black horse. His helmet was up and Jack could see he was an older man; his hair and beard were flecked with gray.

"There's no problem here," said Charles. "Go about your business, old man."

"They won't let us pass. They want to take me somewhere," said Mary.

"I think this is my business," said the knight. He leveled his spear at the two young men. "Begone or I'll run you through."

"Don't make me laugh," sneered Charles. He reached for his sword, but in a flash the older knight's spear was at his throat. "All right, we'll go," said Charles. "But this isn't the end of it. We'll be seeing you again."

After the two had left, the knight said, "You'd better be getting home. I'll accompany you." Once they were safely back at the farm, the knight asked, "Is your mother or father at home?"

"They both died in the plague last year," said Mary.

"I'm sorry," said the knight. "I wish you well." He turned the black horse and rode off in the direction of the forest.

"I'm going to follow him," said Jack.

"Why?"

"I want to find out more about him. Besides, those two hooligans belong to a gang. If they find him I want to help him."

"Jack, you're always dreaming of fighting and of glory. All right, go, but be careful."

Jack knew the forest very well. He followed the trail he thought the knight would take and, sure enough, he soon saw the black horse standing in a clearing by a stream. In a few minutes, the knight came into view. He must have been bathing in the stream because he was bare to the waist. He wasn't muscular but he looked lean and sinewy. Then the two hooligans from earlier, Charles and Ronald, burst into the clearing, waving their swords.

"We told you we'd be seeing you again," said Charles. "Now you'll regret your interference."

"I'm retired from fighting," said the knight. "Just go now and leave me in peace."

Charles laughed. "Not until we've cut you into little bits."

"Enough talking," said Ronald. "Let's have at him."

Jack leaped out from his hiding place, shouting, "Watch out." At the same time, Charles lunged. Suddenly, as if by magic, a sword appeared in the knight's hand. He easily turned aside the lunge, then the sword moved so quickly Jack could hardly see it and Charles' sword went sailing in the air while he looked in disbelief at the wounds he'd suffered in both arms. He turned and ran. His friend Ronald ran after him.

"I though you were unarmed," Jack said. "Where did your sword come from?"

The knight smiled. "Oh, old Jenny is never too far away."

"Jenny?"

"The name of my sword."

"What's your name?"

"You can call me Lan, er, Landry."

"That's a funny name. I came here to warn you. Those two belong to a gang. You'd better leave now. They'll be back looking for revenge."

"I think Jenny and I can take care of those youngsters. But I was going to move on anyway. I'm going to Camelot."

"To Camelot? May I come with you? I can be your squire." He picked up Charles' sword and swung it around. "I can use this. And you can teach me so I'll get better."

"You'd be safer staying home."

"There's nothing for me here. Please take me."

"Let's go to your farm first and see how your sister feels."

"I'm sure she'll agree. Then it's on to Camelot."

"Yes, Camelot."

The Retired Knight and the Young Baron (Winamop)

The door opened a crack and an old woman eyed Jack suspiciously. Jack gave her his most winning smile and said, "I'm Jack, squire to Sir Landry, retired knight. We're on our way to Camelot. Can you perhaps spare some food and water, and water for our horses? We can pay you for your trouble."

The old woman scowled. "I have nothing to spare. Nobody in this parish has anything to spare. The Young Baron has taken it all. If you know what's good for you you'll get away from here as fast as you can before the Young Baron finds you, too." The door closed.

Jack turned to Sir Landry, who was waiting on his black steed, Midnight. (Jack's own horse was short and small; he'd named her Betsy). "Should I break down the door?" he asked.

"No, let her be. We can survive a while longer. Let's see if there's a village nearby."

They continued through farmland that looked as if a blight had descended on it. The fields were empty or nearly empty. Few peasants were about; those who were glared at them as they rode by. Since the passing of King Arthur, Britain has fallen into near anarchy, but this was the worst they'd seen yet.

"Look," Jack cried. "There is a village."

"Yes, and that looks like an inn."

"I'll be glad to see a real bed," said Jack. They'd been sleeping outside on the ground since leaving Jack's village.

They entered a yard in front of the inn. A stable boy came out and said he'd tend to their horses. Jack noticed that two of the yard's fences were partially down. The inn itself looked shabby, as if not kept up for a long time. The entered and were greeted by a middle-aged man who also looked shabby. "Can you put us up for the night?" Sir Landry asked.

"That'll be no trouble. We have no other customers at the moment."

"This area seems to be in sorry condition. Was it the Plague?"

"Yes, the Plague in the person of the Young Baron."

"We've heard of the Young Baron. Who is he and what has he done?"

"The old Baron passed away last year. He left his son under the care of his uncle, Sir Henry. But like many of the youth today, the Young Baron is arrogant and soon pushed his uncle aside, assumed control and assembled a group of other young knights, more like hooligans, I'd say. Since then he's seized the farmers' crops, raised taxes and crushed the peasants and merchants. Anyone who tries to stand up to him gets put into his dungeon."

At that moment, two burly young men in armor came through the front door and confronted the innkeeper. "We're here for your taxes," the larger of the two said.

"But I paid my taxes last month," the innkeeper protested.

"This is a new, added tax."

"But you've taken all I have. I can't pay any more."

The large knight turned to his friend. "It looks the dungeon for our friend here, doesn't it?"

"That's the law. Of course, his inn and any other property will be become the property of the Young Baron."

The large knight grabbed the innkeeper by the neck. Sir Landry said, "Just a minute, please."

The large knight glanced at Sir Landry as if he'd just noticed him. "Stay out of this, old man. It's no business of yours."

Later on Jack thought that he shouldn't have been surprised but even he was amazed that in what seemed like a second Sir Landry had his sword, which he called Jenny, out and pressed to the large knight's throat. "I beg to differ," said Sir Landry. "We intend to stay the night here and we want no harm to come to our host."

"You'll pay for this," said the other knight, who'd drawn his sword but stood uncertainly, not knowing what to do.

"Possibly," said Sir Landry. "Now, the two of you go back and tell the Young Baron that I'll be paying a visit to him tomorrow to discuss this. And, by the way . . ." A lightning move with Jenny and the other knight's sword went flying in the air where Sir Landry deftly caught it. "Now go."

"By all means, pay us a visit," said the large knight. We'll be waiting for you."

Sir Landry raised his sword and the two quickly scurried out. When they were gone, the innkeeper said, "I thank you, but I'm afraid it won't do much good. If you go to the Young Baron's castle, they will be waiting for you, and however skilled you are with the sword you are just one man."

"I'll be there, too," put in Jack. "And I've been learning how to use my sword."

The innkeeper shook his head. Sir Landry smiled and said, "Maybe we won't be the only ones to pay the Young Baron a visit. Now, here's my plan."

*   *   *

The next morning Sir Landry stood outside the gate of the castle. It was a cloudy day. All was quiet, as if this barren area was waiting for something to happen. "I'm Sir Landry, here to see the Young Baron," called out the Retired Knight.

The gate swung open and two dozen armored men marched out. There was another person, an older man dressed in a courtly robe. The knight next to this man lifted his visor, revealing a handsome face suitable for a movie star, although there were no movie stars at the time. "I am the Young Baron. My two tax collectors have told me about you. You've interfered with the laws of my land and must be punished."

"That remains to be seen. Perhaps the laws of the land must be changed."

The older man spoke: "You look familiar, Sir Landry. Have me met, possibly in King Arthur's time?"

"It's possible."

"Enough of this talk," said the Young Baron. "Seize . . ."

Before he could finish, the Retired Knight had jumped off his horse and, before anyone could react, held his sword against the Young Baron's throat. "Don't move," said Sir Landry, "or I'll cheerfully dispose of your master."

"Don't move," the Young Baron gasped out.

"Good. Now hear me out. You have mismanaged your land. You've raised taxes so much the people have nothing left. You've taken all the crops so the farmers are starving. If I hadn't come along, your people would have revolted on their own. If you want to retain your position, you'll return to the policies of your father, reasonable taxes and a only enough of the crops to sustain your men in return for protection against outlaws and other threats." He pressed his sword into the Young Baron's throat.

"Yes, yes, I agree," said the Young Baron. "I'll do everything you say."

Sir Landry withdrew his sword. As soon as he did, the Young Baron cried, "I disavow everything. Seize him. He's just one man."

The armed men moved forward, but the Retired Knight said, "I advise you to look around."

The Young Baron and his men looked. There, arrayed around the castle, were dozens of peasants, also a number of merchants, plus the innkeeper, armed with a variety of weapons—scythes, hammers, logs, poles, even a few rusty spears. They looked menacing, more than ready to attack the armed men and overwhelm them with their numbers. Sir Henry stepped forward. "We accept your terms, Sir Landry," he said.

The Retired Knight looked at the Young Baron, who nodded.

"Watch out," called Jack. One of the knights, the burly tax collector was running at Sir Landry, his sword raised. Two of the other knights stopped him and wrestled him to the ground. It was clear they wanted nothing to do with the mob surrounding them.

"Sir Henry," said the Retired Knight, "I appoint you regent until you think the Young Baron is capable of ruling in a just way, as did his father. Empty your dungeon and return to the people what's theirs. Now it's time for me and my young alert squire to be moving on."

"I'm sure we've met before," said Sir Henry. "This is the bane of becoming old. I can't quite remember."

The Retired Knight smiled. "Maybe one day you will. In the meantime, treat your people well. Jack, let's be off." As Sir Landry and his squire rode off, a little sunshine pierced through the gray clouds.

The Retired Knight and the Princess
(Winamop)

"I don't like this dungeon," I said. "The straw is prickly. It's damp and cold and it stinks."

"You're not supposed to like it, Jack," said Sir Landry, the Retired Knight, whose squire I'd become.

"What are we going to do? When the Prince gets crowned tomorrow he'll probably have us killed."

"It's a long way until tomorrow. Be patient."

Let me go back a little. After leaving the land where Sir Landry had displaced the Young Baron who was abusing his people and put the Baron's sensible uncle in charge we had entered another small kingdom. "I know the ruler here," Sir Landry had said. "I believe he'll be more hospitable than the Young Baron." I had faith in the Retired Knight, but in this instance he had proved to be mistaken.

We could see the castle ahead. As we rode there scores of peasants were also on the pathway, carrying pigs, hens and baskets of fruit. "What's going on?" I asked.

"Don't you know? The old king has died. His son the Prince is receiving the crown tomorrow. There'll be a feast tonight. We've been ordered to bring all of our goods to the castle."

"Won't that be hard on you?" said Sir Landry.

"It will, but we dare not disobey."

We rode through the gate. A knight came out. "Who are you?" he demanded.

"I'm Sir Landry. I was a friend of your king. I was coming to see him but now I hear he is dead and his son the Prince will become king tomorrow. Can we have an audience with the Prince?"

"Wait here." The knight left and returned some minutes later. "Follow me," he said.

We followed him into a large banquet hall. People were scurrying about loading wares on long tables. From the looks of things, the feast being prepared would be enormous. At the head of the hall two figures were seated on thrones. One, I assumed, was the Prince. He was a handsome man with a petulant mouth. He wore a red robe set with many jewels But my eyes were immediately drawn to the woman next to him, in a blue robe, the most beautiful woman I had ever seen, with sparkling emerald eyes and long blonde hair. Sir Landry spoke: "I'm sorry about your father. I had hoped to see him.'

"He was an old man," the Prince said dismissively.

"I don't know if you remember me. I am Sir Landry. You were a small boy when I was here last."

"I think I do remember you, but I recall you under a somewhat different name. No matter. This is my sister, the Princess Anne."

A princess. I should have known. "I remember you well, Sir Landry," she said.

"You may stay for the feast," said the Prince.

*   *   *

I'd expected an enormous feast but this exceeded my expectations. The hall was filled with knights, eating and drinking. We sat at the table with the Prince and Princess. I could not take my eyes off her.

"What are your plans when you become King?" asked Sir Landry.

"I plan to have a good time," said the Prince. "My father was a stick-in-the-mud. Would you believe it, he cared for the welfare of the peasants, as if they didn't exist to serve us?"

"I see. And what do you think of that, Princess Anne."

"Oh, my brother's word is law. After all, I'm just a woman."

"My sister knows her place," said the Prince. "I shall have to marry her off."

Princess Anne looked down at her plate and blushed.

The feast went on. The hall became noisier as the knights became drunker. It was evident that the Prince was also drunk. "Go on," he said to the Princess, let's see you dance. Let the men see your legs."

The Retired Knight stood up. "I don't think that is necessary," he said.

"The Princess will do as I tell her, won't you?"

"Yes, brother."

"You've had too much to drink," Sir Landry told the Prince.

"You dare speak to me like that," said the Prince, pointing to Sir Landry. "Guards, seize that man." He pointed to me. "And that one, too."

We were immediately surrounded. To my surprise, the Retired Knight didn't attempt to draw his sword. When he saw me looking at him he made a gesture for me to be still. "It's all right," he said. So that's how we landed in the dungeon.

*   *   *

I was dozing off when I heard a sound. It was a key in the door to the dungeon. I was immediately awake. The door creaked open. It was the beautiful Princess. "Good evening," said Sir Landry.

"You were expecting me, weren't you?"

"Yes, I was. I thought that the little hellion I knew couldn't have possibly turned into that simpering maiden you were pretending to be."

"I had no choice. My brother took command of the Palace Guard after our father died. It would be a disaster if he took the crown tomorrow. He's already tormenting the peasants and there are rumblings of discontent. And he's a drunken fool."

"I seem to recall him as an unpleasant child."

"Can you help me? I do have my followers among the knights."

"How did you get past the guards?" I blurted out.

"That was no problem. They were passed out from drinking."

"And the Palace Guard?" said Sir Landry.

"The same."

"Then now is the time to strike. Lead us to the Prince's chamber."

As the Princess had said, the guards in front of the Prince's chamber were passed out. One of them stirred and opened his eyes. Sir Landry knocked him unconscious with his sword hilt. We entered the chamber. The Prince was sprawled on his bed, snoring loudly. A young woman, clad only in a shift, was half on top of him. She screamed when she saw us and ran out. The Prince sat upright. "What are you doing here? You should be in the dungeon."

"Sorry to disappoint you."

The Prince reached for his sword by the side of his bed. Sir Landry's sword was instantly at his throat. "Don't make a sound. Do you wish to live?"

The Prince nodded. "Good. You would not make a good king. Get dressed. I'll escort you to the castle gate. You can have your steed. Ride it to the next kingdom. Possibly you can reform and start a new life."

"All right. I will." The Prince stood up, then he suddenly dove for the Princess. He had his arms around her and I didn't know what we would do, then he let out a moan and sank to the floor. The Princess held a knife in her hand. "It was an accident," she said. "He ran into my knife."

Sir Landry examined the Prince. "He's dead."

"I didn't mean to kill him," said the Princess.

"Of course not. No matter. We must prepare for tomorrow."

The next morning the hall was packed with even more people than the night before. The peasants had been allowed in to witness the coronation of their new ruler. Sir Landry stepped forward. "The Prince has suffered an unfortunate accident," he said. "He is dead. The Princess, as the King's remaining child, will rule instead."

The peasants, who'd looked sullen at the prospect of the Prince reigning over them, broke into a cheer The ceremony went on, only with the Princess receiving the crown. That night there was once again feasting but the Princess's followers did not get drunk. I ate and drank my fill. I looked at the head of the table but didn't see the Princess, nor Sir Landry.

Early the next morning the Retired Knight shook me awake and said we'd be leaving. "Where have you been?" I asked.

"That's of no consequence."

"But why are we leaving? We can stay for a while. The Princess likes you."

"Yes, but she likes ruling more."

"But she's so beautiful. You don't think she killed her brother on purpose, do you?"

Sir Landry smiled. "She is beautiful," he said. "And it's best we move on."

I'd learned that the Retired Knight was wise. We packed our things and, before anyone else was awake, were on our way.

Resident of the Month
(Hackwriters)

I was having another drink, trying to relax. I don't know why I was nervous; it was just something for our little retirement community newspaper. When I retired as vice-president in charge of the San Francisco office of the country's fourth largest ad agency I'd moved there. I'd become a pretty avid golfer and the community was built around a golf course. I hadn't planned to do much else, but somehow I got involved in a few of the community's committees, joined a few clubs, then I was elected to the community's Board of Directors and in my second term was made Board president. I suppose I was a prominent member of the community. So it wasn't much of a surprise when someone from our monthly newspaper called and said they'd like to do an article about me. They had a feature they called "Resident of the Month."

I told them "Sure, come on over," and this afternoon was the interview. My doorbell rang at precisely the time we'd set and there was a guy I knew from one of my committees, Paul Lerner, who also wrote for the newspaper. I'd bought one of the larger houses, on the golf course; a bachelor, I lived alone but I liked to have friends in and to have an occasional party there. I invited him into the living room, offered him a chair and also a drink. I still had mine. "No, thank you," he said. "Nice house."

"Thanks. I had some help fixing it up. Well, shoot. What can I tell you?"

"Let's see. You did very well in advertising, I know, became head of your agency's San Francisco office. How did you get there?"

I thought for a moment. "Let's see. I grew up in a small town in upper New York State; you never heard of it. Went to college on a football scholarship."

"I didn't know that."

"Yeah, I was a pretty good fullback. Anyway, after college, I moved to the City, New York City, that is, had no money, stayed at the YMCA. I had three goals, get a job, get my own place to live, get a girl. Well, I got the job at the agency, selling space, was pretty good at it. Got a couple of raises and got an apartment. It was the 60's so there were plenty of willing girls around. You don't have to put that in your story. I was on top of the world. Then the agency offered me a job in their San Francisco office., a promotion. Naturally, I took it. I worked hard and became a vice-president."

"Someone told me you were married?"

"I was, twice, and divorced twice."

"I'm sorry."

"That's okay. Didn't work out. One of my exes helped me decorate the house."

"Okay, let's get to what you've done since moving here." Lerner went on asking questions, covering my golf and all my other activities and of course my being President of the Board of Directors. He wrote everything down in a steno's notebook. Eventually he said, "I guess that about covers it."

"Good," I said, relieved.

"You know," said Lerner, "I think I will have that drink now."

I poured him a drink and another for myself. Lerner looked around and said, "I see you have a lot of books. Funny, with all your activities I wouldn't have taken you for a great reader."

I shrugged. "I did a lot of reading after I retired. You wouldn't believe it but before coming here I was a bit of a recluse, then I decided I'd better get out and start doing things." I didn't mention that I'd also been doing a lot of drinking along with my reading.

We talked about books some more, then Lerner said, "You know, I somehow feel I haven't gotten the entire story about you."

"What do you mean?"

"Well, two marriages that didn't work out, still a bachelor. Do you ever have any regrets?"

I considered, then decided, what the hell, why not? "Yeah, there was a girl, in New York. I said there were a lot of willing ones but she wasn't so willing and naturally this was the one I wanted. By the way, this is all off the record."

"Sure. Go ahead."

"Her name was Marilyn. Not like the others, a sweet girl. She was slender, had big gray eyes, brown hair, soft voice, serious, but when she smiled it was like the sun coming up. I don't know what might have happened if the agency hadn't offered me the job in San Francisco. Who knows, my entire life might have been different. But I was ambitious. I couldn't turn it down. So I said good-bye to Marilyn. She cried."

"Why didn't you ask her to go to California with you?"

"I don't think she would have gone. Anyway, she would have wanted to get married. I was on my way to California, all those San Francisco girls. Marriage wasn't in my game plan at that time. A few years later when I visited New York I asked around about Marilyn. She was married and had kids. I told myself she'd probably had gotten fat. That was the end of that."

"Too bad. Do you still think about her?"

"Nah, that was a long time ago, in a different life."

"I see." Lerner finished his drink. "Thanks. I hope I haven't been too nosy. That's what happens when you're a writer."

"No problem, just don't put in that stuff about, you know."

"I won't. Thanks again."

After he left, I sat and thought for a while. I don't know why I'd told him about Marilyn; maybe the drinks I had, maybe because I'd bottled it up for so long. But I'd lied to him about not thinking about her any more and about having no regrets. I thought about her every day. I regretted losing her every day. I poured myself another drink.

Resident of the Month—II
(Hackwriters)

"He murdered his wife, you know."

The speaker was Ezra Finch, intercepting me as I was on my way to interview his neighbor Horace Cooper for a Resident of the Month story. Ezra was well-known in our California retirement community as a loon. He roamed our streets looking for cars parked illegally and weeds growing in front yards, which he'd then report to our Board. No one had been inside his house for years and I'd hate to imagine what it looked like.

"Thanks for the information, Ezra," I said, continuing on my way.

"I suppose you're interviewing him about his great garden. He may have a nice back yard but he's still a murderer."

"I'll keep that in mind."

Let me explain. Our retirement community's newsletter had a feature called "Resident of the Month," and it was my job to write this. Horace had come to our attention because he'd planted a beautiful garden, which was going to be written up in a regional magazine. As to Ezra Finch's accusation, Horace's first wife Millie had disappeared several years ago and had never been found. The local police of course investigated and naturally Horace was a suspect. They'd dug up his back yard to make sure no body was buried there and had found nothing. Horace had remarried, to a nice lady named Helen, already a resident, who had unfortunately fallen victim to dementia, common enough in our community, and he'd been caring for her the past year.

I rang Horace's bell. He answered and led me out to the back patio, where I'd be able to view his garden, which in fact he'd started after the police had dug up his yard and to which he'd been devoted ever since. If Horace was indeed a murderer he was an unlikely-looking one. He was short with a mild face and blue eyes behind round glasses. His former wife, as I recalled, was a large woman, and they'd been one of those unlikely couples that you wonder about.

The garden, as I saw, was beautiful with roses and other flowers I'd have to ask him to identify, a variety of colors artfully arranged. Horace had prepared a table with cold drinks on it. We sat down and I asked my usual first question: where was he born and brought up, then I led him up to the time when he'd moved to our community and then to the planting of his garden, tactfully avoiding any mention of his first wife. Midway through the interview, his present wife Helen came out on the patio, looking as if she'd just awakened from a nap. She had a pretty face but also the blank eyes of someone with dementia. Horace introduced me and explained why I was there. She said, "That's nice", sat down on a lawn chair and began to softly hum to herself.

We continued with the interview and I learned more than I ever thought possible about flowers and creating a garden. Suddenly Helen said, "I'd like some ice cream, please."

Horace looked at me. "She loves ice cream," he said. "Excuse me for a minute and I'll get her some. It's one of the few pleasures she has left."

"Sure," I said.

When he went inside the house, Helen looked at me and said, "He murdered his wife, you know. He hid the body and then, after the police dug up the yard, he buried her there. He's very clever." Then she resumed her humming.

In a few minutes Horace came out with the ice cream. We ended the interview. I thanked him and he thanked me for coming. I walked back to my house, looked at my notes and considered. Ezra Finch said Horace was a murderer but Ezra was a loon. Helen had told me the same thing and she had dementia. If I went to the police they'd dig up that beautiful garden. There'd be no article in the regional magazine, an article that would reflect well on our community. And what would be the point? Even if Horace had killed his first wife, he'd certainly never harm anyone again. Above all, if Horace was gone, who would take care of Helen? No, I was all for justice being done, but in this case it was best to lie sleeping bodies, if there was one, lie. I went to my computer and started writing my usual "Resident of the Month" story.

The Loan
(Hackwriters)

Paul Lerner put down the phone and went out to the enclosed patio, where his wife Sally was working on a painting. "Who was it?" asked Sally.

"You'll be surprised. It was your son Nick. He and Maria are at the Galleria, shopping, then they're coming to see us." The Galleria, Roseville's premier mall, was about ten minutes away from the Northern California retirement community where Paul and Sally had been living for almost ten years.

"I bet I know what they want." said Sally.

"Maybe they just want to visit us," said Paul.

Sally snorted. "Nick's going to ask you for that loan. I knew it when they announced those furloughs."

Nick, their oldest son, was within three months of his 40th birthday. Like Paul before he retired, he worked for a State of California agency in Sacramento, but he'd advanced much further in the ranks of the state bureaucracy . . . Nick, Paul thought, was a good-looking man, tall, a little over six feet, in good shape because he worked out daily in a health club. Maria, his wife of 15 years, was an attractive woman. Paul knew she was 37 years old, but she could have passed for much younger. She was a fair-skinned blonde with cool blue-gray eyes, also rather tall, slender, with shapely legs. Nick had met her when they both worked in a State office, but Maria hadn't stayed there very long. She'd gotten a job with a non-profit agency their department worked with and now had a high-paying position, or she had until six months ago when the agency, in the economic slump, lost its funding and closed down.

The furloughs for State workers were also a result of the economic slump. The last time they'd seen Nick and Maria, Nick had hinted that, without Maria's salary, they were having a hard time meeting their bills. This wasn't surprising as Maria had persuaded Nick to buy one of the large (and expensive) houses that had been springing up all over the Sacramento area before the housing bubble burst. Sally thought the house was unnecessarily big as Nick and Maria had no children (she held Maria responsible for this) and it came with a large mortgage. Like most of their generation, Nick and Maria liked to live large. Besides the new house, they had two new cars, Maria went for "beauty treatments" every week and Nick's health club was the most expensive in Sacramento.

"You may be right," said Paul. "The furloughs are supposed to cut pay by ten percent."

"Did Nick say anything about Maria's getting a job."

"No. I guess she's still looking."

"I should hope so. And what's she doing shopping when she has no job and Nick's getting a pay cut?"

Paul shrugged. "I've been looking over our finances," he said, "and I think we can swing a loan of $5,000 without disturbing things too much." Paul didn't think that Nick and Maria had any savings to speak of. He knew that Nick had the State's equivalent of a 401k plan but with the collapse of the stock market its value had probably dropped by at least one-half in the past few months. Luckily, Paul, who was of the conservative generation, had put most of their assets in treasury bonds since retiring. They had a modest return, but, as investors who'd lost their money in the stock market had discovered, they were a safe haven in a recession.

"That's a lot. Can we afford it?"

"I think we can."

"Well, we'll see."

*   *   *

Nick and Maria arrived about an hour later. Maria carried several packages plus a bouquet of flowers, which she gave to Sally. She came over to Paul and gave him his usual kiss. In her heels, Paul noted, she was two inches taller than him. When they were seated in the living room, they talked about what they'd been doing since the last time they'd been together. Nick and Maria had been to a concert at Arco arena and to a play downtown. They'd also discovered a new French restaurant.

Paul had been recovering from his annual winter cold and Sally was preparing to have cataract surgery the next month. The Lerners' big male cat, Rascalman, came ambling out and promptly sat in Maria's lap, something that always irked Sally. After a few more minutes of idle talk, Maria said she wanted to show Sally the clothes she'd just bought, which Paul knew would irk Sally even more. Nick asked if he could talk to Paul while the women were occupied. Here it comes, thought Paul. They went out to the enclosed patio and Paul shut the glass door.

"You've heard that they've started the furloughs?" said Nick.

"I read about it in the Bee."

"Things were tight already and that's really going to make it tough. I was wondering if you could make me a loan."

"How much do you think you'll need?"

"I was thinking of something like $10,000."

Paul was taken aback. "$10,000!" he said.

"Well, we've fallen behind on our mortgage payments."

"Why didn't you let me know sooner?"

"I thought we could handle it. We're really trying to cut down. I've given up the health club and Maria is cooking three nights a week."

Great sacrifices, thought Paul. "I assume Maria is still looking for a job?"

"I admit she was a little slow in getting started. She liked being free, as she called it. But she's really started trying."

"Any prospects?"

"You know how tough it is out there. There's one lead. They said they'd call her back, but you know how that is."

"I know. Well, let me think about it and talk it over with your mother."

"It's a lot to ask but I hate to keep asking you for money in dribs and drabs and I figure $10,000 will hold us for six months. Something's bound to happen in that time."

Yes, our new president says things will get even worse. "I'll call you during the week, all right?"

When, after having the coffee and cake that Sally insisted they have, Ken and Maria had left, Paul told her about his conversation with their son. "I knew he'd be asking for a loan."

"You were right about that."

"But $10,000, that's outrageous. We can't afford that."

"We can if I sell some treasury bonds. I was thinking of doing that anyway. They're higher than they've ever been."

"No, I don't want to sell anything. Those bonds are our safety net. Didn't you tell me that?"

"I suppose I did. Why don't I offer to loan them the $5,000 we talked about?"

"That's a lot of money, too. If you think we can afford it, all right. We can't let them get thrown out of their house."

*   *   *

The next week Nick called. Paul picked up the phone; Sally had gone to a club lunch. "Hi, Dad."

"Hi, I was going to call you."

"About the loan . . ."

"Your mother and I talked and we can let you have . . ."

"That's why I'm calling. We don't need a loan any more. Maria got a job, another non-profit. They've just gotten a big grant, one of Obama's things. She'll be getting even more than in her old job."

"When did this happen?"

"Remember that lead I told you about. They did call her back, on Monday. That's why Maria was shopping. She was hoping they'd call her. She went in there Tuesday and wowed them."

"That sounds great. How about the mortgage?"

"Maria got an advance so we can take care of it. Look, I have a meeting. Maria and I are celebrating this weekend, but the next weekend we want to take you and Mom out to dinner."

"All right, I'll let her know. We'll be in touch."

When Sally returned, Paul told her the news. She snorted and said, "It's just like them to go out celebrating even before she starts. When will they ever start saving?"

"We're the saving generation. They're the spending generation."

"They're going to get into real trouble some day. I know it."

"The governments pouring billions of dollars into the economy. Maybe things will get better. Anyway, we have a dinner coming." He'd still set aside the $5,000, just in case.

The Bad Feeling
(Hackwriters)

Paul Lerner awoke with an intense feeling that something bad was going to happen that day. He didn't usually have such feelings. His approach to life, he knew, had always been cautious. He put this down to having grown up in New York with a Jewish mother. Jews had every right to be cautious, having been persecuted through the ages and even now some madman who was president of a county was threatening to wipe them off the map. When he was growing up, his mother was always telling him to put on his hat and coat in the winter, to wear his rubbers if it was raining, not to play too hard during the hot summer. He was cautious, but he didn't think he was unnecessarily fearful. What was coming?

Paul glanced at his bedroom window. It was spring; sunlight was slanting through the blinds. It was going to be a nice day. He was feeling pretty good, no doctor or dentist visits coming up. His wife Sally slept beside him. Their three sons were all employed. Their finances were in order. In the morning, he had a couple of errands—return some books to the library, deposit a check at the bank. In the afternoon, he was scheduled to play golf with his usual foursome. Nothing special, just another day in the life of a retiree. Still, he couldn't shake the feeling that something bad was on the horizon.

At breakfast, Paul asked Sally how she was feeling. "I'm fine," she said. "Why do you ask?"

"Just wanted to check. We haven't heard from any of the boys for a while. Maybe we should give them a call."

"I'm sure they're all right. If not, they would call."

"I suppose so."

"Are *you* all right?" She looked at him quizzically.

"Sure, I'm fine."

But he still had that feeling.

As he dressed, Paul considered that living in a retirement community as they did, bad news was not uncommon: someone coming down with something; a friend or acquaintance in the hospital; every now and then, someone passing away. But right now everyone he knew was in pretty good shape. He wondered how his sister, who still lived in New York, was doing. Maybe he'd give her a call.

At the library, he found some books he liked and the line at the check-out counter was short and moved quickly, no mothers taking out millions of books for their kids, as sometimes happened. In the library parking lot, he looked carefully before backing out. No, no little kids in the way. At the bank, he deposited his check and the teller for once didn't try to get him to open up a savings account or try banking online. He drove home slowly and put the car in the garage without mishap. The morning was over.

Sally was going to lunch with some friends. "Are you driving?" Paul asked.

"No, Carol is picking me up."

"Tell her to drive carefully."

"She's a good driver. Are you sure you're all right?"

"Yes. Have a good lunch."

After he had his own lunch, a sandwich, he called his sister in New York. She was surprised at his call. He said he just wanted to catch up on things. She was feeling fine, the weather was pretty good, nothing unusual going on. They chatted for a while, then Paul said he had to go off and play golf. He still had that feeling.

The three other members of his foursome were Dan Crowley, a retired surgeon, who, as might be expected, played an aggressive game; Hank Whitley, who'd been a financial advisor and whose game, like the stock market, was up and down; and Bob Goolsby, a big guy who'd sold insurance and who was the loudest and most competitive. The foursome had played together for almost six years and were used to ribbing each other, mostly good-naturedly, sometimes not so good-naturedly.

Paul usually played a steady game. He was known for his accurate putter. This afternoon he was paired with Dan against the other two. Paul started off badly; he was distracted by that bad feeling. Pull yourself together, he told himself. You're not going to be hit with a golf ball. He settled down and at the 18th hole they were even. He pitched his fourth shot onto the green and it rolled to within three feet of the hole. "That's a gimme," said Dan. "He never misses those."

"There's always a first time," said Bob. "Hey, I'll bet ten bucks you don't make it."

"I don't want to bet," said Paul.

"Go ahead," said Dan. "Take his money."

"Yeah, go ahead," said Bob. "You're going to blow it."

"Okay," said Paul. He stood over his shot and made sure of his line to the hole. He wasn't nervous at all. Then he saw what he had to do. He hit the ball gently. It slid just past the hole.

"Hah," yelled Bob. "What did I tell you? He choked. Hand over my ten bucks."

Paul knew he'd be taking a ribbing for at least the next few weeks. It would be worth it. This was what primitive people must have felt like, he thought, propitiating the gods. The gods must have been satisfied. The bad thing had happened. The bad feeling had gone away.

A Truly Lousy Day
(Hackwriters)

Paul Lerner awoke with a feeling of dread. Why? Oh, yes, D-Day, the dentist that afternoon. Only a check-up, but it didn't matter. As a child of the Depression (the real one), who'd gone to cut-rate neighborhood dentists when a kid, drill buzzing away, no anesthetics, pain while helpless in the chair, going to the dentist would always be an ordeal. He only hoped no new bad thing would be found with his 80-year old teeth. Also, it had rained the day before, to the delight of the local forecasters, who greeted any type of bad weather as wonderful news. Paul hated to drive in the rain. It was going to be a lousy day.

He saw that his wife Sally was already out of bed; he might as well get up and face the music. As was his habit, he turned on his computer and checked his e-mails. Uh, oh, more bad news. An e-mail from the editor of one of the online magazines that printed his stories saying that he was discontinuing it, a victim of the recession. Paul had somehow become a writer after his retirement, doing articles for his local paper, then for a senior paper, and also short stories for online magazines. As it happened, the editor of another one of his magazines had put it on hiatus because of the death of her husband. Another one, once out monthly, now came out quarterly. His markets were drying up.

When Paul told Sally he was losing markets for his stories, she told him he should start looking for some others. His wife was always sensible. After breakfast, he checked the calendar. He had to bring his car in for a smog check and they also wanted to get their annual flu shots. You'd think that being retired they had all the time in the world to do such things, but Sally had something doing every day the next week: chorus practice, lunch, bridge game, who knew what else. Paul wanted to get the smog and flu shots done because no rain was forecast next week. He asked Sally again (they'd discussed this already) if there was any day she could go. Sally was sensible, but she had a family trait, no one in her family could reach a quick decision. They went back and forth over this again until finally Paul lost his temper (he was feeling edgy anyway) and said, "For Christ sakes, just pick one day so we can get it done." Sally agreed she could miss one chorus practice so they'd go on that day, but she wasn't happy and Paul knew he could look forward to chilly relations for a while. The lousy day was getting lousier.

Paul didn't feel very much like going out (it was still raining), but he had some errands to run: the library, the bank, the supermarket. At the library, he couldn't find a decent book; he finally took a novel he'd once read but a long time ago. He couldn't bear to have nothing to read; it made him physically uneasy. He had to stand on a long line with mothers and their kids, all taking out millions of books; this didn't make him any happier.

The line at the bank wasn't as bad, but there were four windows and only two tellers. He could see other bank people standing around seemingly with nothing to do. Why not have one be a teller when people were waiting? When he finally reached a window he deposited the check for his monthly senior paper column. He also asked the teller, a young woman, for his current balance. "All right, Paul," she said. Paul? He didn't know they were on such friendly terms. He hated it when young people called him by his first name. She gave him the slip with his balance on it, a few thousand dollars, and asked, "Paul, are you comfortable with all that money in one place?"

They had a bill due for painting their house, the reason for the large balance, but what business was it of this snippy young woman? "Yes, I'm comfortable," he replied. He took his slip, turned around and left. When he got back into his car, he realized that was the second time that morning he'd lost his temper. He considered himself a pretty laid-back person and usually he was. It was the impending dental appointment. The news about the online magazine didn't help. Neither did the weather.

After lunch, a light one as he had no appetite, Paul drove to the dentist. As on cue, the rain became harder and at one point he could barely see ahead. He drove slowly and of course the driver behind honked his horn. Idiot! That's why people had accidents. Finally, he reached the dental office, late, but as usual he had to wait anyway. That was obligatory. And as usual his apprehension mounted as he waited. Once in the chair, he felt as if pinned down with no control over what happened to him. Olga, the dental hygienist, was another young woman, conscientious but talkative. While she scaled his teeth she carried on a one-sided conversation, telling him about her new apartment, her new dog, her planned vacation in Hawaii. Occasionally, she asked him a question, such as "Had he traveled anywhere recently himself?" He could only grunt an answer.

When the cleaning was finally done, seeming to have taken forever, his dentist, Dr. Barrow, came in for a look. Barrow was a large, beefy man, always cheerful. He poked about in Paul's mouth, saying "Uh, uh. Uh, uh" What did that mean? A cavity? A crumbling bridge? The dentist straightened up and said, "You're holding your own. Surprised that one tooth hasn't broken, just a filling. See you in another few months." Paul breathed the proverbial sigh of relief, feeling much happier already. Maybe it wasn't such a lousy day after all.

As if in keeping with Paul's new mood, when he exited the dental building the gray skies had given way to blue and the sun was shining. Driving back was much better. It helped to see. His route always took him past a MacDonald's. Sally like their milkshakes. He stopped and got her one, strawberry, her favorite. When he reached home, he gave it to her; it was a peace offering. "How was your check-up?" she asked.

"The old guy is holding his own."

"Good. Feeling better?"

"Much better."

The rest of the day went by uneventfully. After watching the TV news—the "storm" had passed, the forecaster sounded disappointed—they retired to bed. Paul as usual kissed Sally, then turned over. As was his habit, he reviewed the events of the day. It had started badly but ended okay. Maybe, like that tooth that was supposed to have crumbled, he'd hang on for a while. He'd try to think of a story to send in for the online magazine that was closing down. It was a good magazine and he wanted to be in its last issue.

The Lie
(Hackwriters)

Paul Lerner was alone in his house, which was in a retirement community near Sacramento, California. It was mid-afternoon. The house was quiet. His wife Sally was off visiting her sister. The cats were sleeping. He himself had been leafing through a magazine and was ready to fall asleep.

The phone rang. Probably one of those computer calls, Paul told himself. No, it was a neighbor, Lila Silverman. She knew Sally was away and was inviting him to a little party they were having on Sunday. The Silvermans were great party givers. Sunday? That was pro football day and Paul remembered the 49ers were having an important game. Besides, there was Lila's husband Conrad, the golf bore. Paul knew that if he came Conrad would immediately latch onto him and describe his latest round of golf, hole by hole. He said the first thing that came into his mind. "I'd like to but I have, uh, a cold, a bad cold."

"Oh, that's too bad. You better stay home and take care of yourself."

"Yes, I will." Paul breathed a sigh of relief. Later, he would think that if he hadn't been half-asleep he'd have come up with a better excuse, like just saying he had a previous engagement, that wouldn't have led to such complications.

Paul spent a happy Sunday afternoon watching an exciting game, won by the 49ers on a last-minute field goal. On Monday, his doorbell rang. It was Lila Silverman, bringing him a big bowl of chicken noodle soup. "I knew Sally wouldn't be home yet," she said. "How are you feeling?"

"Uh, better, yes, better." He gave a cough, which he hoped sounded convincing. He took the soup Lila stayed for a while, then left, telling him to take care and to call her if he needed anything. Paul felt guilty but not too guilty. He would have hated to have missed that game.

Later that day Paul's phone rang. It was his sister Eunice, who lived in Sacramento. "I heard you weren't feeling too good," she said.

"Where did you hear that?"

"Lila Silverman called me. I can't make it today but I'll drive over tomorrow and stay until Sally gets back. I know you can't take care of yourself."

"I can manage perfectly well."

"Ha!" Eunice was Paul's younger sister, but she'd always regarded Paul as being helpless. She was recently divorced and had two teen-aged children, a boy and a girl. She'd gotten a nice divorce settlement and had quit her job. Maybe she had time on her hands, thought Paul.

"Look, you don't have to come. It's only a cold. I'll be fine." Wait, he didn't even have a cold.

"That's not what Lila told me. She said you looked terrible. I'll see you tomorrow."

Paul put down the phone. Looked terrible? What had he started?

That night Paul's sister told her two teen-agers that she'd be visiting their Uncle Paul for a few days. She was trusting them to behave while she was gone. No parties in the house. The kids assured her they'd be as good as gold.

*   *   *

"This is delicious," said Tom Baldwin. Tom was Paul's best friend and his tennis partner. He'd come to visit Paul in the late afternoon and Eunice had of course invited him to stay for dinner.

"Thank you," said Eunice.

"Not only pretty but a good cook. Paul is lucky to have you so close by."

Paulo saw Eunice blush. She was still an attractive woman. Tom was a widower and lived by himself. He had long ago told Paul he had no intention of ever marrying again. Was this resolve weakening?

"Paul is lucky to have such a good friend," said Eunice.

Oh, no, thought Paul. What was going on here?

"So you're feeling better?" Tom asked Paul.

"I feel fine." He'd always felt fine.

"So you can play in the tournament this weekend?"

Paul had forgotten about the tournament. The retirement community had an active tennis club. "Yes, I suppose so."

"You don't want to over-exert yourself," said Eunice.

Again, Paul felt guilty. All this concern and he'd never really been sick. "I'll be okay," he said.

Tom lingered after dinner. He and Eunice discussed movies, television, politics, travel. They seemed to share the same taste in everything. Was a senior citizen romance blooming? The last thing he needed, thought Paul, was to have his bossy younger sister move here and tell him what to do all the time.

Meanwhile, in Sacramento, Mary's two teenagers were busy texting their friends that their mother would be away and they had the house to themselves. They'd promised their mother no parties but what was the harm in having a few friends come over Of course their friends texted their friends who in turn texted their friends.

Sally returned that Friday and Eunice left. She understood that Sally would take over the care of Paul. Her work was done. Paul confessed to Sally that he'd told a little fib to get out of going to the Silvermans the Sunday before. She said he should be ashamed of himself. He also told her of the sparks he thought had been struck between Tom and Eunice. Sally said it would be wonderful if the two, one widowed and the other divorced, could get together.

Paul and Tom finished runner-ups in the tournament. The Silvermans were there as spectators. Afterward, Lila came up to him and said he seemed to have recovered very quickly.

"Yes, I was lucky." Again, Paul felt a little stab of guilt.

Lila gave him a skeptical look. "I'm glad Sally is back. I'll give her a call."

"Yes, good." He saw Conrad Silverman coming over. "Uh, I have to be going," he said, moving quickly away.

Eunice returned home. Her kids had tried to straighten things out but the house was still in a mess. She yelled at them and they tried to make excuses, eventually retreating to their rooms. Eunice sat down. She really needed a man in the house, she thought. Although she'd just come back, she wanted to get away. She called Tom Baldwin, who was happy to hear from her.

Sally told Paul that Lila had called and they were going over for a little party the next Sunday. The 49ers were having another important game but he'd have to miss it. Later that week Eunice called and said she'd be visiting Tom that weekend and that she'd see them at the Silvermans' party, to which they'd been invited. She told Paul she really liked Tom. Paul's heart sank. His throat felt scratchy and his nose was stopping up. He was coming down with a cold. It was no use. He couldn't give the same excuse again. He'd have to go to the party.

The Coward
(Hackwriters)

Since grade school, Tom Newberry knew he was a coward. It wasn't anything he did but what he didn't do. He was studious, got good marks and was well-behaved but was also a good athlete and too big to be an obvious target for the school bullies. His best friend, Walter Potter, was also studious, got good marks and was well-behaved but was unfortunate enough to be small and look somewhat like a weasel. He was also something of a wise-ass. It happened in the fifth grade. Walter mouthed off to Mike Butler, the largest kid in their class and not one to anger. Mike told Walter he'd see him after classes in the schoolyard and teach him a lesson. Tom went directly home after his last class. He told himself that nothing too bad could happen. If there was a fight, certainly one of the teachers would intervene. He had a lot of homework to do and couldn't waste his time.

Afterward Tom learned that it *had* been pretty bad. Mike had smacked Walter around and then pinned him to the ground. No teacher was around to intervene and Walter wasn't too popular with the other kids so they actually urged Mike on. He twisted Walter's arm until Walter had cried "Uncle" before Mike let him up, then he'd hit Walter a few more hard blows for good measure. Walter hadn't come to school the next day and the next week Tom heard that his parents had moved him to another school. Tom knew he should have been there for Walter that day. He also knew he hadn't been because he was afraid of fighting Mike Butler. He was a coward.

*　　*　　*

As a man, Tom was still studious and mild-mannered and still pretty athletic, playing tennis on weekends. He lived in the suburbs with his wife Alice and they had a five-year-old daughter Mellisa. He had a well-paying job as a computer programmer and was able to work at home once a week. Alice worked as a librarian. On this day she'd suggested that if he had the time Tom could take Mellisa to their local playground in the afternoon. Tom thought he'd done enough work by three and it was a nice sunny day so off they went.

Tom pushed Mellisa on the swing for a while until she got tired of it. She said she wanted to play in the sandbox. She'd brought her pail and shovel. "All right," Tom told her. He sat on one of the benches. The playground was pretty crowded. A lot of mothers sat on benches, also a few fathers. The sun on his face felt good. He could hear birds chirping off in the distance. It was all very peaceful. There was a loud scream from the sandbox. It was Melissa. Tom ran over as quickly as he could. Melissa was crying. He bent over her. "What's the matter, honey?"

"That boy threw sand in my eyes."

Tom looked up and saw a pudgy boy of about six standing nearby. He looked defiant. "Did you throw sand in my daughter's eyes?" Tom asked him.

"So what if I did? She's a sissy."

"That was a bad thing to do. You should say you're sorry."

"No way. She's a little crybaby."

Tom felt defeated. "Come on," he said to Melissa. "Let's go. I'll buy you an ice cream."

He took Melissa by the hand and turned to go but found his path blocked. It was a young man, maybe 25, a little smaller than him but muscular and with a sneer on his face. He wore a sleeveless shirt and had tattoos on his arms. "What's the idea of yelling at my kid?" he said.

"I didn't yell," said Tom reasonably. "He threw sand in my daughter's face. I just asked him to apologize."

"I didn't throw any sand," said the boy. "She hit me."

"Maybe your kid should apologize," said the tattooed man.

"He's a liar," said Melissa.

"Hey, who you calling a liar?" said the man.

This whole thing was getting out of hand, thought Tom. He looked around and could see that all of the mothers were watching. "Look, why don't we just forget about this?" he said. "Come on, Melissa, let's go."

"He's a bad man," said Melissa. "You have to fight him."

"No, that's not the way. Fighting doesn't solve anything."

"He's a sissy, too," said the tattooed man. He pushed Tom in the chest. It didn't really hurt. "Come, Melissa, we're going."

"Daddy, he pushed you," cried Melissa.

"It's all right. It was nothing. Let's go."

The tattooed man laughed. He pushed Tom harder, causing him to go back a few steps.

"Daddy, don't let him push you." Melissa grabbed hold of the tattooed man's leg. He pushed her away.

He touched her, thought Tom. He touched my daughter. He had no idea of what happened next. He'd heard of people seeing red and that's what he saw now. He heard a buzzing in his ears. Then he heard shouts. Then he felt hands pulling at him. The tattooed man was on the ground and Tom was on top of him, hitting him. "That's enough. I think he's learned his lesson." It was one of the other fathers talking.

Tom stood up. His fists felt bruised and he was breathing heavily. "That kid's a bully," said one of the mothers. "So's his father. Thank you."

"You beat him up, Daddy," said Melissa. "You're a hero."

"Well, I think we better go," said Tom.

When Alice returned from the library, Melissa immediately ran up to her, shouting, "Daddy's a hero. That bad kid threw sand in my eyes and that bad man pushed me so Daddy beat him up."

"What? Tom, you beat somebody up."

"Not really, just a little shoving match." He described to Alice what had happened.

"Well, that guy sounds like a real jerk. You did what you had to do."

"Nobody will bother me again," said Melissa. "Daddy is a hero. He'll beat him up."

"No, fighting is still not the right way."

"But you won't let anyone push me."

"No, nobody is going to push you."

That night in bed Tom pictured the whole playground incident in his mind. He knew that he'd just wanted to avoid conflict, get away. He didn't know what had come over him. He guessed some primitive instinct that caused parents to protect their children. Well, he wasn't a hero and he'd still rather walk away than fight. But he wasn't a coward, not when it came to his daughter, and that made him feel pretty good.

The Bubbly Girl
(Winamop)

I was coming off a tempestuous affair with the writer Patricia Dowling when I met Barbara Hastings. Barbara was also a writer, but of a completely different kind. Patricia wrote long, dramatic novels while Barbara had just published her first book, entitled, "If You Believe It, You Can." It was at one of those publishing parties in New York. The crowd was noisy, drinking as much of the publisher's liquor as they could while exchanging the usual literary gossip. I spotted a young girl at the far end of the room, pretty, blonde, nice figure, being chatted up by an aging novelist known for long-winded historical sagas and also for his attempts to seduce anyone he came across.

I pushed my way through and introduced myself. The latest in my detective series had recently appeared and the blonde recognized my name. She told me her name and I recognized it. Someone hailed the aging novelist. He said self-importantly, "I have to see my publisher," and disappeared into the crowd. Good, I had Barbara to myself. "You know your friend's reputation?" I said. "You should be careful around him."

"Oh, he's harmless. His last book didn't do well so he needed a little cheering up."

"I see. Do you really believe that if you believe it, you can?"

She smiled; I was to find out that Barbara smiled almost all the time. "Yes, I do."

"I wish I did." I was in a dry period, I didn't know the cause, maybe because of my recent break-up. I had a contract for the next book in my detective series and had no idea what I was going to write. Maybe that's why I was attracted to an optimist like Barbara.

"I can see you could also do with a bit of cheering up," she said.

"I do. Maybe you're the one who can do it. Shall we get out of here and go to my apartment?"

"I didn't mean that kind of cheering up. I know. Meet me tomorrow. I have an idea."

* * *

I met Barbara at Columbus Circle, at the southern tip of Central Park. "All right," I said. "What's your idea/"

"Follow me." She took my arm and I allowed her to lead me. In a few minutes, we entered the Central Park zoo. The zoo; I hadn't been there since I was a kid. It was one of those nice New York summer days, not hot or humid, the sky a mild blue, the trees a peaceful green background. The nice weather had brought out a lot of families, people milled about, kids shouted, everyone seemed to be having a good time.

Barbara took us to the seals' pond first. We watched the seals' antics as they contested for fish thrown to them, barking and flapping away. Then we went to the big cats building, tigers pacing back and forth, lions mostly sleeping. After that, to see the elephants, majestic and tranquil. I have to admit I was feeling more cheerful. We had hot dogs from a stand and they tasted wonderful. "Well, are you feeling better?" Barbara asked.

"I am. This was a good idea."

"I looked through one of your books," said Barbara. "Your detective is pretty cynical. I suspect he reflects the way you feel about life. You have to start expecting things to get better, not worse. You have to believe in yourself. Let yourself be happy."

Her enthusiasm was somehow touching. "I'll try, as long as you keep teaching me." I leaned down and kissed her. She responded. This time she did come to my apartment. I can truthfully say that after her visit I was feeling, if not happy, a lot better about life.

*   *   *

The next few weeks with Barbara sped by. We went to all of those places in New York where a couple could have a good time: museums, outdoor cafes, the theater, picnics in the park. One day we even went to Coney Island, ignored the tackiness, went on the rides, played the silly games (I won Barbara a stuffed bear), had cotton candy. Barbara was at her bubbliest. "Isn't this a hoot?" she said.

It was. It was also bound to end. I'd begun to write again and it was hard to get back into the shoes of my cynical detective while feeling so upbeat all the time. Also, Barbara's relentless cheerfulness began to get on my nerves. "Look, the sun is out," she'd say. "It's going to be another lovely day."

"The forecast says it'll be almost 100 degrees."

"Then we can go to the beach."

"We'll fry there. If we're sensible, we'll stay right here with the air-conditioner on high."

"All right. I can write another chapter of my book."

That was also irksome. She'd already gotten a nice advance for her second book and she was able to churn out words effortlessly. Of course, what she wrote was sheer nonsense, but the publisher, and the public, thought it was the wisdom of the ages, leading to success and happiness. In fact, her title was, "How to Be Happy and Successful in a Recession." I was a slow writer, no matter how I was feeling, and it was irritating to look over and see her merrily typing away.

What led to my breaking off with her was something else. I happened to be in midtown on some errand or other. I passed the outdoor café Barbara and I liked to go to and there she was, with the aging novelist I'd first seen her with. They were holding hands across the table and she was smiling at him. Maybe she was still cheering him up. Whatever it was I decided that I'd had enough of the "just believe and everything will be fine" life; I was going back to normal. When I told Barbara I thought we should stop seeing each other she wasn't fazed at all. "All right," she said. "If that's what you want. But if you ever get down again let me know." And with that she bubbled her way out.

Shortly after that my former girl friend Patricia Dowling called me and suggested we go out for drinks. We did and agreed to give it another try, this time taking it slow and easy. I didn't know if this was possible with Pat but so far we've managed and she hasn't thrown any lamps at me. We recently attended still another one of those Manhattan publisher's parties and there was Barbara Hastings. But she wasn't with the washed-up novelist, she was with a young guy who, I was told, had just written a best-selling book called "Times are Tough but Never Give Up." They were smiling and laughing, both bubbling over with good cheer.

Pat nudged me. "Yes, I see them," I said. "I think Barbara has found her match."

"Yes," said Pat. "But imagine what their children will be like."

Uncle Warren and Aunt Edie
(Hackwriters)

Uncle Warren

"I'll have a second helping of that," said my Uncle Warren.

My mother put another pile of beef stroganoff on his plate. She knew this was his favorite and that's why she'd made it. Uncle Warren had been invited to this dinner because my father wanted to ask him for a favor. Uncle Warren, my father's older brother by a few years, was the success of the family. He was one of the officers of a financial company in Sacramento. My father had been considered a modest success, that is, until last year, when the Recession had forced him to close down the small advertising agency he'd formed. He hadn't been able to find a regular job since so I guess that maybe now he'd be looked upon as a failure. I'm not sure how my Aunt Edie, the younger sister, was viewed, not as a great success; she was a schoolteacher in Sacramento and, now in her mid-forties, an old maid.

Uncle Warren finally finished eating, the table was cleared and my father led him outside to the patio. It was time to ask for the favor. I ran back up to my room, which was almost directly over the patio. I opened the window and listened. "You know we've been stretched pretty thin since I had to close the agency," my father said.

"You haven't been able to find anything since then?"

"The ad business isn't big in Sacramento. I've had a few consulting jobs; in fact, I have a pretty good one now. They've helped. But no, nothing on a regular basis. It's not that we're broke, but Ken's ready for college this fall and we just don't have enough to pay for it."

Ken? That was me. I didn't know I was the subject of this favor. I'd been accepted to UC Berkeley. My father hadn't discussed this with me but I knew UC Berkeley, even though it was a public university, had gotten pretty expensive. I wish he'd spoken to me. I was ready to go to our local community college. I knew times were tough.

"UC Berkeley, right?" said Uncle Warren. "That's a good school."

"I know. It's also expensive. I need a loan. I'd pay it back as soon as I could, of course."

"I wish I could give you something, but I'm pretty strapped myself. Don't let this get around but the firm isn't in that good a shape. This damn Recession. It doesn't look as if it'll ever go away."

"Oh. I thought you were doing okay. I'm sorry I asked."

"That's all right. I wish I could help."

Aunt Edie

So that was that. During that week, I did talk with my father about what would happen in the fall. I told him I was ready to go to our community college. I also went around to the local fast food places and put in applications. My father said he still hoped to find a job, things were bound to get better.

That Saturday afternoon my father and I were watching a Cal football game on TV. The doorbell rang. "I'll get it," I said. It was my Aunt Edie. She usually came over once or twice a month but always called first. What was up?

"I'm sorry to drop in without calling," said Aunt Edie, "but I just talked to your Uncle Warren and thought I'd come over. Is your father in?"

I led her into the living room. "Edie! What a surprise! A pleasant one."

I liked my Aunt Edie. She might have been plain-looking but she had a nice smile. She'd always been interested in what I was doing and talked to me as if I was a grown-up, not just a kid. "I'll come to the point. I've heard Ken might not be able to go to UC Berkeley. That would be a shame. I think he has a promising future." She reached into her handbag and handed a piece of paper to my father. It was a check; from the way my father looked at it. a large check. "I don't know what to say?" my father exclaimed.

"Then don't say anything."

"But can you afford this?"

"If I couldn't I wouldn't be giving it to you."

"But you're just a . . ." my father stopped.

"Yes, just a schoolteacher. But I have a good head for money. That's why I never listened to what Warren advised. I made some good investments, and now I've made another one, in Kenneth." She looked at her watch. "I have to use your bathroom. I've asked someone to meet me here. If he comes, can you let him in?"

"Sure," said my father. He looked at me. "Well, your Aunt Edie is full of surprises. I think there's a lot we don't know about her."

In a few minutes, Aunt Edie was back. I saw she's put on some make-up, lipstick and rouge, and had loosened her hair . . . I'd never seen her like that before and she looked almost pretty. "You look very nice, Aunt Edie," I told her.

The doorbell rang. "Oh," Aunt Edie said. "That must be Nelson. I asked him to meet me here. We're going to an early dinner and then to a concert."

"Nelson?" my father said.

"Yes, Nelson, my friend. Do let him in."

I snapped out of my trance and ran to the door. Nelson was an imposing gentleman of about fifty. He had a broad, handsome face, ruddy, with gray hair and a gray moustache. He came in and Aunt Edie gave him a quick hug. She introduced us, then said they must be going. My father looked as if he'd been struck by a thunderbolt. "Well," he said, after they'd gone. "There's another surprise."

So that's how I came to be attending UC Berkeley this fall. I worked at a MacDonald's over the summer so had enough money to buy Aunt Edie a nice present when she announced she and Nelson were getting married. Oh, yes, the company my father was doing the consulting job for hired him as advertising manager so our family's personal recession was over.

A Suburban Story
(Winamop)

A shooting in our nice quiet suburb just outside of California's capital, staid Sacramento? Yes, it happened. Well, maybe our suburb wasn't that nice or that quiet. It was the seventies; we were all young couples; the sixties had ended all sexual inhibitions. Consider one of our many summer barbeques. The women were all made up, nicely tanned, wearing light dresses or shorts. The men eyed them appreciatively. Husbands danced with wives, not necessarily their own. Looks were exchanged; maybe notes were passed. There was a buzz of gossip. Who was seeing whom? After the barbeque, there'd be arguments; at the end of the summer there'd be break-ups. Before year's end possibly there'd be a divorce. No, a shooting wasn't that impossible. Maybe it was inevitable.

I myself tried to keep clear of our group's flirtations, maneuverings and gossip. I'd been married to Sally for six years. We had two small children. Our sex life had dwindled, but that was as expected. I was working hard to get a promotion at my office. We needed the money to take care of our house and the kids. My time of playing around was over; at least that's what I told myself.

Much of our group's gossip centered around my next-door neighbor and tennis partner Sidney Edwards. This was first because Sid was an unattached male, divorced the year before. He was also tall, ruggedly handsome and, as far as women were concerned, a charmer. And he was a successful lawyer. It wasn't that Sid boasted of his exploits; he was quite discreet. But several times, when I was up early to get the morning paper, I caught a glimpse of a woman hurriedly leaving his house, undoubtedly to return to her own home and husband.

The latest rumor going around was that Miranda Fairchild was having an affair. Miranda wasn't a beauty but was attractive in a quiet way, or so I'd always thought. She was tall, slender, dark with raven-black hair and eyes that suggested a depth beyond her suburban housewifely exterior. I especially liked her quiet voice. Her husband Kenneth would seem to be a likely cuckold, pale, prim, nerdish-looking with glasses, some kind of accountant, absorbed in his work. They were childless. You might say this was a pairing where the wife was almost certain to become the object of some other man's desire.

I won't go into the details of all the speculation about Miranda and Sid, which went on for some months. Everyone in our group was sure they were having an affair. At one of our get-togethers, one of the other wives was blunt enough to corner Sid and ask him outright. He denied it. No one believed him.

On this autumn Saturday, I was at Sid's. We'd finished a morning's tennis and I'd stopped in for a beer. We were sitting in his living room. The TV was on, a college football game. Someone came through the door (Sid always left it open) and burst into the living room. It was Kenneth Fairchild. He was even paler than usual and shaking. Pointing a finger at Sid, he said, "I know about you and Miranda."

"Calm down, Kenneth. There's nothing to know."

"You lying bastard. You've been screwing my wife. Don't try to get out of it."

"I assure you, Kenneth, that's not true. Come on, I'll get you a beer."

"You think you can talk your way out of anything. Not this time." This wasn't the nerdish Kenneth Fairchild we knew. He had a crazy look in his eyes. Then he pulled out a gun and pointed it at Sid.

"Kenneth, don't be foolish. Put that down"

Sid started to get up out of his chair. Kenneth fired, one, two, three times. Then he dropped the gun and started crying.

*   *   *

I won't keep you in suspense. Ken was shaking so badly that only one shot hit Sid, in the shoulder. It went clear through. The other two shots went into the wall. Sid recovered in a few months and is back playing tennis. He refused to bring charges. The Fairchilds moved away and no one knows where they are. Sid of course was, as he'd said all along, not the one having an affair with Miranda. As you'll have guessed, I was the guilty party. I didn't mean to be unfaithful, but I couldn't resist that soft voice telling me everything would be all right as I poured out my troubles to her. My wife Sally, I'm happy to say, never suspected anything. I got my promotion and things were easier after that. Sid never again went near any of the other wives. I think he might get married, to another attorney in his firm. The shooting made a big stir in our neighborhood for a while, but now things have calmed down, and life in the suburbs goes on.

Lucy PC
(Hackwriters)

I was a little surprised when our ten-year old son Greg suddenly developed an interest in the environment shortly after entering the fifth grade. "Dad, what are you doing?" he said to me after I'd tossed a couple of used batteries into the wastebasket. "Don't you know that will poison the earth? You have to put those in a special place. We have one at school."

"All right," I said. "By all means, take them to the school."

The next night at dinner Greg looked at his plate and said, "We're not eating this, are we?"

"What's wrong?" asked my wife Sally. "It's fried chicken, one of your favorites."

"Don't you know how they treat chickens?" demanded Greg. "They cram them in those cages like, uh, um, well, chickens. It's animal cruelty."

"You never worried about how chickens were treated before," said Sally.

"Yeah, well, I do now. It's inhuman. Or inhumane. Anyway, it's a crime the way we treat animals. As a matter of fact, I think I'm going to become a vegan."

"A what?"

"A vegan. Someone who eats vegetables."

"Well," said Sally, "don't expect me to change the way I cook just because you've gotten some strange ideas."

"They're not strange," said Gregg. "I was just ignorant before. I don't want to eat chicken any more. But as long as you cooked this I guess I'll finish it."

After Greg stalked to his room, Sally asked, "What's gotten into him?"

"I don't know. Maybe it's some class in school."

The mystery was solved the next day when Greg came home with a new girl in his class. Her name was Lucy and her family had moved to Sacramento from San Francisco. Her father, she immediately told us, was a Deputy Director of some State agency. In other words, a bigwig. I should mention that I'm a community college teacher, definitely not a bigwig. Sally worked part-time as a teacher's aide to supplement our income.

Lucy was a pretty girl, with dark hair, a firm chin and piercing black eyes. I could see why Greg was taken with her. When Greg told her I taught at the community college, she at once asked if we had a Women's Study program. "No, we don't" I told her. "We have to have more practical courscs."

"What's more practical than informing your students about women's role in society? After centuries of male oppression, we're finally coming into our own."

"True," I said. And she was a good example of that. Somehow I suspected what her next question would be and, sure enough, she asked, "What about Black Studies?"

"No, we don't have that either, but we do have a lot of black, uh, African-American students."

"Huh!" was her response to that. "Greg told me you belong to a swim and tennis club. Do you have any African-American members?"

"Hmmm. I think we do have a few. It's a neighborhood club and not too many African-Americans live around here."

"Housing discrimination," she said triumphantly.

I was glad when Greg interrupted this inquisition by telling Lucy he wanted to show her his room. They went upstairs and I was left to wonder what Greg had gotten himself into.

What it was became apparent in the next few weeks. Greg put up posters in his room showing endangered whales, polar bears, tigers, wolves and many other species. Almost every day after school he went with Lucy to some meeting or other to promote a worthy world-saving cause. One afternoon he was in a protest organized by Lucy against the unhealthy lunches the school was serving. On another occasion, he and Lucy joined a protest in front of city hall on behalf of the homeless. When they weren't doing all these things Greg was at Lucy's house or she was at our house, plotting strategy, I suppose.

One day I remarked to Greg that his girl friend Lucy was really into PC.

"What's PC?" he asked.

"PC is for politically correct. It's something that's swept over our society in the last, oh, maybe ten years. It means you have to believe men oppress women, everyone oppresses black people, rich nations exploit poor ones, we're polluting the earth and humans are destroying the animals, all the stuff that I'm sure Lucy has told you about."

"Yeah, she has. She knows a lot. Anyway, she's not my girl friend."

"She's not? You're together so much I thought she was."

"Yeah, I know. We do all these things together, but she won't say that she's my girl friend. She says I have to prove myself more. I don't know what more I can do."

"I'm sorry to hear that," I said. "She's a very pretty girl. She's also has some pretty decided views."

"Yeah," said Greg. "But I think I have an idea."

The next week Greg brought home someone else, an African-American boy named Bryant Clark. He said Bryant was his new friend. Bryant was a tall, handsome boy with a confident air. His father taught, not at a mere community collage, but at UC Davis, where he was a department chair. His mother was a lawyer. Evidently, Greg had lured him to our house with the promise of showing him some new video games. They went upstairs but were soon back down, with Bryant saying, "Those games suck."

"I'm sorry," said Greg. "Do you just want to hang out?"

"No, I have better things to do."

"I'll see you at school tomorrow."

"Maybe," said Bryant. "Maybe not." Then he was gone.

"Your new friend didn't seem too friendly," I said.

"Yeah. He can be pretty snooty. The only reason I asked him over here was to show Lucy I wasn't a racist."

"Why should she think you're a racist?"

"I don't know. She says I still have to overcome my bourgeois, or something, upbringing. Anyway, I invited Bryant over so maybe she'll say we can officially be a couple." He sounded hopeful.

But a few evenings later Greg came to dinner looking glum. "What's the matter?" I asked.

"It's Lucy," said Sally.

"You're still not an official couple?"

"Worse," said Greg. "I introduced her to Bryant, to show her, you know, how I'm not a racist, and now she's with him all the time."

"Too bad," I said. "I know you really liked her."

"Yeah." Then he brightened up. "But, you know, like you said, she had some pretty decided views. And some of them were pretty far out. Mom, do you think you can make fried chicken tomorrow night?"

"So you're no longer a vegan?"

"No, I think I was just going through a phase."

Yes, I thought, a PC Lucy phase. It was just as well he'd passed through that. I just hoped the next phase wouldn't be going to the other extreme.

My Friend Dennis
(Winamop)

It was a lazy Sunday morning. My wife Ellen and I were finishing our coffees while reading sections of the New York Times, which we subscribed to although we now lived in a suburban section of Sacramento, capital of California. The doorbell rang. "Who can that be?" said Ellen.

"I'll go see." I opened the door. It was Dennis Crown, showing up as usual with no warning.

"I have a meeting in San Francisco tomorrow so I thought I'd stop by and see how you guys are doing. I hope it's not a bad time."

"No, come on in. It's Dennis," I called out to Ellen.

She came out to the hall and Dennis gave her a big hug and a kiss on the cheek. "You're looking as pretty as ever," he said, as he always did. As she always did, Ellen blushed.

I should explain that Dennis and I had been roommates at a New England college about 20 years ago, something I always thought was due to a clerical mistake as I was a scholarship student and he came from a wealthy family. After college we'd gone our separate ways, I winding up as a civil servant and Dennis as a kind of dealer who traveled the world obtaining art objects for wealthy clients. Every now and then, as now, he'd drop in unannounced.

We returned to the living room. Ellen made some fresh coffee and Dennis filled us in on his adventures since we'd last seen him. As well as being rich, he was handsome and charming. His stories always involved clever doings to get some precious art object as well as a beautiful woman he'd get involved with. The women were always alluring but in the end he'd leave them no matter how much he was attracted to them. His latest adventure had been in Russia and, if you believed him, he barely got away with a famous painting, eluding capture by the KGB with the help of a beautiful woman called Titiania. He'd been sorely tempted, he told us, to take Titiana back with him; he'd really fallen for her. "It's sad. She was the most desirable woman I've ever known. But you know how much I value my freedom. I can't be tied down. I suppose I'm a confirmed bachelor and will end up all alone. I sometimes envy you two. Your life may be, well, predictable but you have each other."

"You meant to say 'boring,' didn't you?" I said.

Dennis just laughed. He asked about our son and daughter, now both in college. When they were younger, he'd always brought presents for them. "Hard to believe they've grown up," he said. "I don't suppose I'll ever have children either." He put on a wistful look. It was my turn to laugh.

Eventually we arranged for Dennis to stay over for two nights. He'd go to his San Francisco meeting the next day, Monday. As it happened, I also had a meeting, at the Sacramento airport hotel, on Tuesday. He'd take Ellen out to lunch and shopping, he told her. Then he'd have to leave, flying to Hawaii. And he meant to take us out to dinner that night. We could name our restaurant. There was no question Dennis brought a little excitement to our predictable suburban lives.

When we prepared to go to dinner I noticed that Ellen had put on a dress; she usually wore a shirt and jeans. She had also put on more make-up than usual. "You look very nice," I told her.

"You noticed?"

"Yes. What do you mean by that?"

"Nothing. Let's go. Dennis will be waiting."

Dennis of course told Ellen she looked beautiful. All during dinner, he directed his attention to her, asking her preferences as to the menu and the wine, complimenting her taste. I put it down to his automatically exerting his charm on any woman within his range. When we returned and were going to bed I remarked that Dennis was outdoing himself tonight.

"What do you mean?"

"Well, all of that telling you how beautiful you look, how great your taste in wine is, how he wished he'd met a woman like you earlier, you know, his usual charm offensive."

"I thought he was being very nice. You could use a little of that charm yourself."

"Come on. Do I have to smother you with complements all the time?"

"Some of the time wouldn't be too bad. Anyway, let's not quarrel. It's too late."

Quarrel? I didn't know we were having one.

When I returned from my airport meeting the next afternoon I saw that Dennis's suitcase was in the hallway. It appeared that he was ready to leave. Dennis and Ellen were in the living room. He was holding her hand. "I have to catch an earlier plane," he said to me. "We were just saying good-bye. I have a taxi coming."

"I see," I said. Then it hit me, the way Ellen was looking at him. I knew they'd been together. My heart dropped. "I'll help you with your bags," I said.

Once outside I put down the suitcase I was carrying. The desolation I'd initially felt had been replaced by rage. Dennis faced me with a questioning look. I hit him as hard as I could in the jaw. He went down to the ground. "I think you know what that's for," I said.

He was rubbing his jaw. "I'm sorry," he said. "All my fault. It was only that one time. You don't know how sexy Ellen is."

I went back inside, still in a rage. It must have showed on my face. "What's the matter?" asked Ellen.

"You know," I said. "Dennis. How could you?"

"I don't know. It just happened."

She held her hands up in front of her face, as if to protect it from my hitting her. I could easily have done so. Then, in a minute, my rage vanished and I saw Ellen as Dennis must have seen her, lovely and desirable. No, I didn't ravish her right then and there, nor did we have make-up sex later. It took us a long time to work things out, but in the end we did.

As for Dennis, for a time he seemed to have dropped off the earth. Then perhaps six months later we received a call from him. It was from Russia. He and I spent some time saying sorry to each other, he for Ellen and me for hitting him. Then he said, "Maybe when you hit me it knocked some sense into me. I went back to Russia to get Titania. We're getting married. And we're going to have kids."

Ellen and I looked at each other and we both laughed.

The Success of George Brewster
(Winamop)

When the small market research firm I worked for in San Francisco suddenly went bankrupt I was unemployed for three months before getting a job as an "analyst" with the State's Department of Employment. I was a little apprehensive at being a government employee but Mike McGee, the head of my small section, which dealt with unemployment rates, seemed capable and my fellow analysts seemed like normal enough guys. There was one exception, George Brewster. He was a man in his mid-thirties, short and chubby, who also seemed a nice enough guy but who was clearly incompetent at his job.

Brewster tried but analyzing data was clearly beyond him and he invariably came up with the wrong conclusions or had to ask someone else to explain the numbers to him. He also had the bad habit of transposing figures, which didn't help. He was clearly a drag on the section, as I found out first-hand when he and I were assigned to the same project and I would up doing almost all of the work myself. I asked why George was kept on and was told that it was almost impossible to fire a State worker. Also, McGee had tried many times to get George transferred to another section, but word had spread and nobody else wanted him.

There was one way, however, to get rid of an incompetent employee within the State system. An opening in the department's Sacramento office had come up, a promotion. McGee wrote an enthusiastic recommendation and the unsuspecting office soon had a new section chief. The efficiency of our section went up exponentially and none of us worried about what would happen in the department's far-off office in Sacramento. A couple of years later I myself transferred to the state capital, where most agencies were headquartered, a promotion that I'd earned, I hoped, but for which I'd had to move over to the State's Department of Health.

One day I overheard two of my co-workers talking about a section chief in the Department of Employment of even more than the usual State incompetence. Curious, I asked what his name was and, not to my complete surprise, it was George Brewster. I related my experiences with George and they told me that several reports George's section had put out were so bad the agency director had to disavow them.

Life went on its usual course. I married and my wife and I bought a house in a Sacramento suburb. We started a family. Expenses went up and I badly wanted a promotion, but times were hard and a hiring freeze was on. The next I heard of George Brewster came from a story in the newspaper about a State scandal. From what I understood, a Division chief in the Department of Mental Health had retired and the Employment Department had solved its problems with George by somehow moving him over to the vacancy, another promotion.

The story didn't say so outright but strongly suggested the Division had a responsible Assistant Chief and that she actually took care of things so that George couldn't cause too much trouble. This worked for a few years but then the Division had to select a computer firm to re-design its information system and, under George's guidance, the firm had completely botched the job. Lawsuits were threatened and the State evidently stood to lose millions of dollars. Good grief! I thought. What a mess. I wondered what would happen to George now.

I inquired but never did find out until some years later. I was sent by the Department Director (by this time I'd finally received a promotion) to deliver an urgent report directly to the Director of the Mental Health Department. I made the delivery and when I was leaving the Director's large office I noticed a small cubicle next to it and glimpsed a figure who seemed familiar. I looked in and there was a small plump man with graying hair. "George?" I asked.

He smiled and, to my surprise, said my name. He invited me to sit down. I asked what he was doing. He told me he'd been a Division Chief but had run into a spot of trouble so he'd been moved next to the Director's office in the newly created position of Special Assistant. It wasn't exactly a promotion but he had received a slight pay raise. His job was to review Department memos. He told me that he wasn't too busy but he didn't mind this as he was nearing retirement. "I've had a successful career," he said, "so I'll get a nice pension. Every now and then I calculate it. I'm not sure what I'll do but I might get an RV and drive around the country. It'll be nice to relax after having worked hard all these years. It's time to let the younger people take over the load." He said he was glad to see me and that I should drop in any time.

I went back to may own office, a little larger than George's but not by much, and reflected. I'd also calculated my pension and had a long way to go. Yes, George had had a satisfactory State career. Unconsciously, he'd found the key to getting promoted, be so incompetent that it was the only way to get rid of him. It didn't seem right but, as somebody had said, life wasn't fair. I wished George a happy retirement in his RV.

The Max Von Sydow Connection
(Winamop)

I have a friend here in our retirement community, Paul Lerner, who's by way of being a writer. He writes for a senior newspaper we get and also writes short stories for an online magazine with a funny name, mop-something. I mention this because I guess being a writer explains why he has a wild imagination and comes up with these crazy ideas. The other day, after our weekly chess game, he asked, "Have you ever heard of a Swedish actor, Max Von Sydow?"

"The name sounds familiar," I answered.

"He started in Ingmar Bergman's films. In "Seventh Seal," he was a knight who plays chess with the devil."

"I don't think I saw that one."

"Anyway he went to Hollywood and he's made a lot of movies, some good and a lot not so good."

"So, what about him?"

"Did I tell you I bought an iPad last month?"

"Yes, several times."

"Right. One of the apps I got was Netflix. You know I'm a Woody Allen fan."

"I've seen some of his movies. Pretty funny."

"Yes, his early films were comedies. Then he wanted to do more serious ones, like Ingmar Bergman's. Netflix had a very good documentary on Woody Allen's career on the iPad. After I watched that I naturally became interested in Ingmar Bergman's movies and I found out some of his early ones were on Netflix on the iPad so I watched them and the leading man was . . ."

"Max Von Sydow."

"Right. A very young Max Von Sydow. In fact, I looked it up; he's about the same ago as we are.'

"Pretty old. So what about it?"

"A couple of nights ago we watched a movie on TV, not from Netflix; I think we recorded it from one of the cable channels. It was called "Incredibly Close and Very Noisy." It's about a boy whose father is killed on 9/11. There's an old guy in it, the boy's grandfather. The actor who played him was . . ."

"Max Von Sydow."

"Right again. A much older Max Von Sydow."

"Okay, I'm still waiting."

"The movie is really about atonement. The boy didn't take a phone call from his father so his mother never got a chance to say good-bye. In the movie, the boy searches for people who might have known his father, driven by guilt. He finally tells his mother at the end. The thing is that I've been meaning to call my cousin in New York. We had a fight, I can't even remember about what, and we haven't spoken in years. Seeing that movie made we realize we aren't getting any younger and I'd better do something before it was too late."

"How do you know he's still alive?"

"I called my sister. She's still in contact with him and she had his phone number."

"So you called him and you kissed and made up."

"No, I called and got his answering machine so I left a message."

"Has he called back?"

"Not yet?"

"That's it?"

"That's it, for now. But you don't get the point. It took all of those seemingly random events to get me to make that phone call. Watching that Woody Allen documentary. Watching those early Ingmar Bergman movies. Seeing Max Von Sydow in that movie about 9/11. Even, going back further, getting an iPad."

"But those are just things that happened."

"As I said, seemingly random events. But, you see, the harmony of the universe was disturbed because of the discord between myself and my cousin. It had to be restored and those not-so-random events saw to it that it was."

"Harmony of the universe?"

"Yes. It's a philosophical tenet."

"If you say so."

We left it at that, but the thing is that my wife and I watched an episode in a TV miniseries, the Tudors, last night. It's one of those historical dramas with lots of conspiracies, betrayals, violence and sex. When they ran the cast of characters I saw that one of the actors was Max Von Sydow, This reminded me of Paul and his cousin and this reminded me that I had a situation like that of my own. It wasn't that I'd had a fight with someone years ago, but I had a good friend living in San Francisco and I guess you'd say we'd had a cooling off. I'd been meaning to call him for, oh, I guess a couple of years. I looked and found I had his phone number. I'll try to get him tomorrow. I wouldn't want to disrupt the harmony of the universe, right?

My Cecily Infatuation
(Hackwriters)

Ah, the stupid things we do when we are young. I wasn't that young actually, 25 when I came to San Francisco from New York City, got a job as researcher in an ad agency, fell in with a gang of young people, mostly UC Berkeley grads, because I knew one of them from the Army, started going to parties and became infatuated with Cecile Thornton. Cecile was a secretary at my ad agency, a dark beauty, sexy and provocative, and she knew it. She became one of the gang because she was a friend of Ginny Brewster, then the girl friend of my Army friend Ray Foxbridge.

The Berkeley gang, as I thought of them, usually got together on Fridays after work, meeting in a downtown bar. Someone always knew of a party going on that night. The next morning, Saturday, we'd reconvene someplace, often the Buena Vista, and then go somewhere, possibly over the Golden Gate Bridge to Sausalito or to Sam's in Tiburon. A lot of drinking was done over the weekend and, I'm sure, a lot of sexual activity went on. I was kidded because I drank very little, one reason being that I didn't feel I had the income to squander on alcohol. I was also, I'm sorry to say, a non-participant in the sexual activity. I was known as Ray's serious friend from New York, sober and close with money.

When I think back, I see myself as a minor character in a movie where the sexy heroine has a host of young men waiting on her until she goes off with the handsome hero. I was one of those young men. I don't mean that I obviously lusted after Cecile. When we were all together I'd just say hello, ask her how her job was going and maybe exchange a little gossip about our ad agency. But, on the rare times I caught her alone, I'd ask her if she'd like to have dinner; she'd always say she'd love to but couldn't because she was always busy. I had a few dates with one or another of the girls in the gang, but these always came to nothing. They were nice girls but I was fixated on Cecile.

At work I waited for a glimpse of her or occasionally I'd stop by her desk. At a party I tried to keep her in sight; usually she was surrounded by other guys. At night I thought about her and pictured us together. I was supposed to be serious and sensible and I knew my infatuation was ridiculous but I couldn't help myself. It was if someone had put me under a spell and I couldn't break it.

Then one day I thought I might have made a breakthrough. It was a wedding, Ray and Ginny were getting married. The entire Berkeley gang was of course there. At around seven in the evening, the reception began to break up. Ray and Ginny vanished, off to wherever they were going on their honeymoon. I was about to leave when Cecile came up to me. Her date had passed out drunk; would I be able to drive her home? I'd bought an old rattletrap of a car but thought it could handle that. I said I'd be glad to. Cecile's look made it clear what she thought of my car but she got in anyway. I took a deep breath and suggested we stop somewhere for dinner. She seemed reluctant, then finally named a restaurant near her apartment. I was elated. I was taking her out, not exactly a date but close enough.

The restaurant near Cecile's apartment, as it turned out, was quite expensive, and, as I should have expected, she selected one of the most expensive entrees on the menu. I selected the least expensive, saying I'd had plenty to eat at the reception. I wanted to tell Cecile a little something about myself but it was evident she wasn't much interested. However, she wasn't reluctant to talk about herself. She seemed to spend a lot of weekends going out of town, to Lake Tahoe, to Carmel, to Big Sur, even to places in Southern California. She mentioned names like Lloyd, who was our agency's creative director, and Stan, who I gathered was some kind of local radio celebrity, who'd take her to these places. It wasn't a very encouraging conversation.

When we finished our meal, I had barely enough money to cover the bill. I drove her to her apartment. Before I could say anything at her door she thanked me for dinner, said she was tired and had to get to bed as Lloyd, or maybe it was Stan, would be picking her up early the next morning. At this point, I should have realized my infatuation was getting me nowhere but of course when I got to bed that night I thought of all the witty things I might have said at dinner and I conjured up an entirely different ending to the night.

Several weekends later the gang went to Lake Tahoe. The parents of one of the girls had a cabin we could stay in. Lloyd and Stan must have been busy that weekend because Cecile came with us. We arrived in the early afternoon, had lunch, then went to the beach. Cecile wore a fairly modest one-piece bathing suit but it revealed all of her curves. I could hardly take my eyes off her. That night, we went to one of the casinos, had a buffet dinner, then it was off to the gambling tables. Most of the others played blackjack. I hadn't planned to gamble at all but then I saw a roulette wheel. I'd played some roulette when I was in the Army in Europe so I thought I'd give it a try. This was before the minimum bet was at least five dollars; I think you could play with a minimum of a dollar, so I wouldn't have to bet a lot.

I'd read about systems for roulette and of course knew the classic system of playing red or black, doubling up on your bets, and eventually, at 50/50 odds you'd win. The only problem was that it was possible to have a long string of either red or black and also since the wheel had a zero and double-zero the odds were less than 50-50. In any case I bet on the red or black in small amounts and occasionally on one the four numbers containing my age, 25, and my sister's age, 23. Amazingly, this seemed to be a night when those numbers came up often and after a while I had a sizeable number of chips.

I felt that someone had come up behind me and I recognized the scent; it was Cecile. "I didn't know you were a gambler," she whispered.

"I'm not," I said. "Maybe I should quit now while I'm ahead."

"No," she said. "You're on a lucky run. Go for broke."

"All right," I said. I was caught up in the fever of the game, and of trying to impress Cecile. I pushed all of my chips onto the zero/double-zero. They hadn't come up all night. I could feel Cecile's warm body against mine. Her gaze was fixed on the wheel. Her lips were slightly parted. She too was caught up. The croupier started the wheel . . . The ball went around and around, hit off one side and then the other. Then it settled into the zero/double-zero. I had won, how much I had no idea but it was a lot. The croupier looked at me questioningly. Did I want to leave my chips on the zero/double zero?

"Isn't this is exciting," Cecile said breathlessly into my ear. "Leave them all one. Take a chance. Then we can celebrate."

I took this last to be an invitation. If I won again I'd have a fortune, a small fortune anyway. And I'd have Cecile. "Go on," she said. "Be a man. Do it."

Then it was if the fever broke. I knew the odds against the zero/double-zero coming up again were astronomical. The money I already had would make a big difference in my life. I motioned to the croupier to give me my winnings. There was a collective sigh among the people who'd been watching. Without looking around I gathered up my chips and took them to the cashier. I didn't know where Cecile had gone. Our cabin wasn't far from the casino. I walked there and lay down on my bed. I was drained.

The next day, Sunday, we all went to the beach again. I looked at Cecile in her swimsuit and felt nothing. When the fever of the game had broken so had my infatuation. It was one thing to take a risk but to then double up on that risk was foolhardy. Pursuing Cecile, as I knew all along, could only lead to disaster.

I used my roulette winnings to buy a new car. Later that year I changed jobs and lost track of Cecile. Then someone from the old gang told me she'd married creative director Lloyd but then had divorced him after six months, getting a nice settlement. I was sure somebody else would be next. Whenever I thought of my Cecile infatuation I breathed a sigh of relief.

Buying the House
(Hackwriters)

Tim Holcomb opened his eyes, saw sunlight slanting through the blinds and knew what he'd be doing that Saturday. It was the 1960's and down in Berkeley students were busy taking over the university as they rioted against the evil establishment. But up here in staid Sacramento he and his wife Amy, along with other young marrieds, would be searching for their first house in the suburbs.

Tim looked over at his wife, sleeping with her mouth slightly open, her round face with no make-up looking child-like. They'd met in San Francisco three years ago and after six months had married. Tim worked for the State, an analyst, and after a year they'd moved to Sacramento, where almost all the State agencies were headquartered, so he could get a promotion. Amy was a nurse and she'd had no trouble getting a job in the county hospital. Their move was not only so Tim could be promoted; they also wanted to buy a house, and houses in Sacramento were much more affordable than those in San Francisco. Buying a house, as Tim knew, was a prelude to starting a family. And that was what scared him.

Amy stirred and opened her eyes. "What time is it?" she asked.

Tim told her it was almost nine.

"Already? We better get going." She jumped out of bed. Tim also got out of bed, much more slowly. The Sunday routine had begun. While they had breakfast, Amy pored over the real estate section of the *Sacramento Bee*. Sunday was when open houses were listed. Amy finished marking ads and said, "I think three or four are good possibilities. They're all in Carmichael, in that area we liked."

She passed the paper over to Tim, who looked at the marked ads. "They look okay," he said., knowing he didn't sound too enthusiastic. They'd spent the last six Sundays looking at open houses, except for one weekend when Tim had insisted they take a time out and they went to San Francisco to visit their old haunts. During that time, Amy had seen several houses she liked, but each time Tim had found some fault with them. One was inexpensive but would have needed a lot of repair work and he was no handyman. One house was okay but the back yard was small and if, as they would, have kids there'd be no room for them to play. One house was fine but Tim wasn't sure they could afford the mortgage.

Time was aware that he was putting up a rear guard fight; he justified his actions by telling himself, and Amy, that a house would be their most important investment and they shouldn't rush into anything. He knew the real reason was that he was afraid of what would come after buying a house: the kids, the lawns to be mowed, the crabgrass, the furniture to be bought, the leaking faucets, the broken pipes, the kids, the end of life as he knew it. He'd enjoyed being married, the late weekend mornings, the easy sex, the outings with friends, the trips back to San Francisco or up to Tahoe whenever they wanted to. What was wrong with him wanting to continue that a little while longer?

The first two houses they went to were busts; even Amy hadn't liked them. The saying is that the third time is the charm and Tim had a feeling, even before they entered the house, that this might be the one. It was an older house and the rooms were on the small side, but they could see that it had been kept up. The kitchen appliances were new. The rugs were new. It had been recently painted. Even the air-conditioner, a must in Sacramento, was less than five years old. The real estate lady, a Ms. Sims, led them through the house and Amy was already placing furniture, which they'd have to buy, in each one. The bed would go there, the dresser there. In the living room, that would be the perfect place for the TV. There was a family room off the living room, fine for the kids. The back yard wasn't that big; still, there was room for kids to play.

The only catch, Tim thought, would be the price. The current owners, Ms. Sims said, were in their sixties and were moving to Colorado to be with their children and grandchildren. Their asking price was very reasonable. Tim did the math in his head. Yes, they could get a 30-year mortgage and could meet the monthly payments. Still, he couldn't bring himself to say "Yes." It was too much of a life-changing decision. Let's sleep on it tonight, he told Amy, and then decide. Ms. Sims pointed out that someone else might put in an offer before then. Real estate agents always said that; besides, they could always make a higher offer. Amy finally agreed. Ms. Sims gave them her card. "It has my office and my home number," she told them. "You can call me at any time." A real go-getter, thought Tim. "We'll call you," said Amy. "No later than tomorrow."

*   *   *

What was he doing here? Tim asked himself? Here was a bar in downtown Sacramento. Of course first thing that morning Amy had wanted to talk about the house. He'd put her off, saying he'd miss his bus and that he'd call her at work. All day long he stewed about what to do. It had seemed a good idea, after all that agonizing, to go out for a drink after work with a couple of the younger analysts, just one drink. Then he'd get the bus back. Somehow he'd had more than one drink and he'd heard himself telling the young guys, both unmarried, to have a good time while they could. A couple of girls had come over to their table but now they were gone. Tim knew he was drunk, just slightly, and that he'd missed his bus. God, what was Amy thinking. One of the guys said he'd drive Tim back home; he lived not far away. "Thanks," said Tim. "I have to make a phone call first, okay."

On the drive back, Tim dozed a little. He felt fairly sober now. He knew he'd been an idiot. He'd been acting as irresponsibly as those kids down in Berkeley. It was time to grow up. He was dropped off and as soon as he got through the door, sure enough, Amy pounced on him. "Where have you been? I was worried sick."

"We had to work late, special project."

"Why didn't you call me?"

"I was going to. The time slipped away."

"You smell of alcohol."

"One of the guys wanted to go out for a drink. To celebrate finishing the project. After, he drove me home."

"You were supposed to call me about the house. Now it's probably already been sold."

"No it wasn't. I called Ms. Sims. It's okay. We bought the house. She's coming over tomorrow night with the papers. She's a real go-getter."

"We bought the house?"

"Yes, I just told you."

She rushed over and crushed him in a hug, then she sniffed. "I think you had more than just one beer."

"Maybe. I guess I was celebrating the house, too."

"Come on. Sit down and I'll heat up your supper. We have a lot to talk about."

"I know," said Tim. Buying the furniture, mowing the lawns, the crabgrass, the house repairs, the kids, the end of life as he knew it.

The Bicycle
(Clever Magazine)

All of this happened on my first job with the State of California in Sacramento.

It started with our Division Chief Dennis Rathbone bursting out of his office, even more red-faced than usual, and yelling, "Those idiots. They've screwed me." I knew that this was the day that Rathbone had ordered the Division to have a going-away party for Alistair Fairweather, our retiring Executive Director, so I assumed his explosion had something to do with that. I was right. Fairweather, a tall, bony man of 65 with the aristocratic look and manner of an Executive Director, was also an avid environmentalist and fitness freak who rode a bicycle everywhere. As a parting gift, Rathbone had ordered all Division employees to contribute toward the purchase of a new specially equipped bicycle, which was supposed to be delivered that day. Now it seemed that something had delayed delivery and the bicycle wouldn't arrive. It was no secret that Rathbone was going all out for this occasion because he badly wanted to become the next Executive Director himself. Now his great plans, or at least his great gift, had apparently been spoiled. "Damnit," he repeated. "They've screwed me."

But all was not lost. Henry Watson, Rathbone's assistant, came trotting out after him. "I have an idea," he said. "Let's have someone draw a big picture of a bicycle. We can put it on an easel, cover it up, then unveil it as a surprise."

Rathbone stopped ranting and considered. "That's not a bad idea," he said. He looked around. "Anyone here a decent artist?"

There was no response. "Come on," he said. "Someone must be able to draw a bicycle. How about you, Babcock?"

Babcock was one of the Division's section chiefs. He knew that Rathbone's question was really an order "All right," he said. "I can try."

"Do better than that," said Rathbone. "I have a magazine with a picture of the bicycle so you can copy it. And get started right away. We don't have much time."

We all returned to our appointed tasks while Babcock got a big sheet of drawing paper. About an hour later we heard him moaning and groaning. I can't do this," he said. He threw down the pen he was using. We got up and looked. His picture was a mess. "Rathbone's going to kill me," Babcock said.

"I'll do it." It was Claire Simmons, one of our analysts. She was an attractive girl, I should say woman, who was also smart, a graduate of UC Berkeley. The rumor was that Rathbone had hit on her, as he had with most of the women on his staff. It was said she'd threatened him with a charge of sexual harassment if he didn't behave himself. "I had some art classes in college."

"Thanks, Claire," said Babcock. "You've saved my life."

The party started at noon. The long table in our conference room was covered with dishes from a catering service Rathbone had hired, with money contributed by Division employees. In one corner was the picture, on an easel and covered with a cloth. The room was crowded. Rathbone had invited all the other Division chiefs. Retiring Executive Director Fairweather stood close to the easel. As I've said, he looked aristocratic; he was also said to be vain and overbearing. His wife, also thin and boney and likewise said to be vain and overbearing, stood next to him. Rathbone, heavy and red-faced, was next to them. Assistant Chief Watson stood in the background.

Rathbone began his speech, a flowery oration about what a great leader Fairweather had been. He went on and on and I could see that most of the audience, including myself, had stopped listening about halfway through. Then came the big moment. He tore the cloth off the easel and the picture was unveiled. There was a collective gasp. I could well believe Claire Simmons had taken some art classes; the picture was excellent. She'd drawn a fine-looking bicycle. She'd also drawn riding the bicycle an unmistakable caricature of Fairweather, in a short-sleeved shirt and shorts, his bony elbows and knees protruding, gray hair flying out, whiskers on his chin, a wild-looking old geezer.

Mrs. Fairweather was the first to speak. "How dare you?" she said, looking directly at Rathbone. "How dare you?" She grabbed her husband by the elbow and marched him out of the room.

Rathbone could only sputter, then he said, "Babcock, where are you? You're fired."

Claire Simmons said, "Don't blame Babcock. I was the one who drew the picture."

Rathbone sputtered some more but said nothing. My guess was that Claire's threat of a sexual harassment charge kept him silent. Meanwhile, people, looking at the picture, began to laugh. It was pretty funny. Henry Watson stepped in. "There's lots of good food on the table," he said. "Paid for by everyone. Why don't we all have lunch?" And so we did.

In the aftermath of what I'd always think of as the big bicycle fiasco Rathbone wasn't dismissed but was given a demotion to the Department's office in Stockton. Henry Watson took his place. It occurred to me that the picture might have been a scheme between Watson and Claire Simmons, but soon after she took a job in another Division. Babcock retired in a year. The Division was a much better place to work in under Watson so I stayed on and was duly promoted. A friend of the Governor was brought in to be Executive Director. The big bicycle fiasco became an office legend.

One Last Drink
(Hackwriters)

Paul Weiss glanced at his watch and lit a cigarette. He was sitting at the bar. It was almost eight on a January night in San Francisco. Outside it was cold and foggy. The bar was a small one, a neighborhood place where people stopped in for a drink after work. Right now Paul was the only one there.

Jim, the bartender, brought Paul his drink, a whiskey sour. "Since when did you start smoking again?" he asked Paul

"Since now."

"She's late, huh?"

"Yeah, women are always late."

"Not Carol. Seems to me you're usually the one who's late. She working today?"

"Yeah, you know her. She had to go in."

"How long you two been coming in here?"

"I don't know. About a year."

"Too bad about her father. Is he still in the hospital?"

"Yeah, but he's out of danger now."

Jim swabbed the counter with a towel. "What was it, a heart attack?"

"Yeah."

"How old's he?"

"Not that old, about sixty."

"Well, I can see why she thinks she has to go back home."

"Yeah, but he's better now."

"Still, who knows. Anyway, she'll be coming back."

"You think so?"

"Sure. What the hell, either he gets better or he dies, right? Then she comes back."

"Yeah, then she comes back."

Paul heard the door to the bar open. He turned around and saw Carol coming in, still in her nurse's uniform, carrying her coat over her arm. As always when he saw her, he thought, What a great-looking girl. She was in her late twenties, blonde and fair-skinned, with flushed cheeks. She seemed to bring with her a glow that lit up the dark bar.

She walked quickly up to Paul and gave him a light kiss. "Hi," she said. "Sorry I'm late."

"Had a long day?"

"Yes. There were a lot of good-byes." She looked at his cigarette, burning in an ashtray. "You're not smoking again, are you?"

"Why not?"

"Because it'll kill you, that's why." She picked up the cigarette and ground it out.

Jim asked Carol if she was ready for a drink. "Whiskey sour?"

"Yes, thanks, Jim."

They took their drinks and sat down at a table furthest from the door. Paul said, "I'm glad you came."

Carol gave a little shrug. "Well, one last drink," she said.

"I didn't want you to leave without seeing you after last night," Paul said.

"Last night was something, wasn't it? Our big fight."

"Look, whatever I said, I didn't mean it."

"Yes, you did. But it's all right."

"Have you heard anything new about your dad?"

"Yes, this morning. They think he'll be able to go home in a few days."

"That's good news. But I suppose you're still going."

"Yes, I told you. I wouldn't feel right if I didn't go."

"Yeah, you told me."

"Someone will have to be there to take care of him."

"And it has to be you."

"Paul, I'm going. Don't make it any harder."

"Okay, you're going. Have I told you I'll miss you?"

"You've told me. I'll miss you, too."

"Well, watch out for the bears."

"The bears?"

"Sure, the bears. Don't the bears come down from the hills in Minnesota when it's winter?"

"Yes, I forgot about that."

Paul looked down at his drink, as if the answer to some important question was contained there. "You know," he said, "about getting married. Well, I could think about it."

"Wow, you must really think you'll miss me. But you know you're only saying that because you don't want me to go."

"You're right. I don't want you to go. Don't go."

"Paul, you know I'm going. Maybe you'll be relieved when I'm gone."

"Relieved? Why>"

"Well, you won't have to worry about getting married."

"I told you, I'm willing to think about it."

"And moving out of the city?"

"Why would you want to move out to the sticks?"

"The suburbs, not the sticks. And what about having kids?"

"Maybe there won't be any kids."

"Then why get married?"

Paul shook his head in exasperation. "Christ, why can't you be a self-respecting feminist like everyone else? How did I find the one girl in San Francisco who wants to be married and have kids?"

"Just your luck, I guess."

"Well, look. We can talk about all those things when you get back, right?"

"Yes, when I get back."

Paul didn't like the flat tone in which she said that. "You are coming back? I mean, when your dad's okay. Then you'll be coming back, right?"

"I told you. I can't give any guarantees. I'll have to see how he does. Don't let's argue over this again."

Paul was ready to resume the argument but she was giving him her level look, mouth and chin stubborn. "Okay," he said. "No guarantees." He saw that she'd finished her whiskey sour. "How about another drink?"

She shook her head. "No, I better not. We've had our one last drink. I should go. I have to finish packing." She stood up and went to the bar. Paul followed her. "Well, goodbye, Jim," she said to the bartender.

"So long," said Jim. "Don't take any wooden nickels."

"I won't." She put on her coat.

Paul said, "You'll call me when you get there?"

"Are you going to be worried?"

"Yeah, I'll be worried."

"I'll call."

"And you'll write? Tell me all about life on the farm?"

"It's not a farm, just a place out in the country."

"Okay, write me about life out in the country." He took a step toward her and reached for her arm. "Come on, I'll walk you to your car."

She took a step back and said, "No, it's right outside."

Paul stopped abruptly. "Okay. How about tomorrow? Do you want me to drive you to the airport?"

"No, you'll have to go to work. I'll take a taxi."

"Okay. Well, good-bye then." Before she could say anything, Paul moved quickly forward, embraced her and kissed her on the lips. "Christ, I'm going to miss you," he whispered in her ear. She let him hold her for a moment, then she broke away and went to the door. Before she went out, she turned and waved,

"So long, kiddo," said Jim.

"No wooden nickels, Jim." Then she was gone.

"I guess she's not coming back," said Jim.

"No," said Paul. "I guess not." He lit a cigarette. "Better give me another drink.".

Another Drink
(Hackwriters)

Paul Weiss went into the bar. It was seven o'clock on an unusually warm weekday evening in San Francisco. The bar, a neighborhood one, was almost empty; too early for the regulars. Paul sat on a stool. Jim the bartender came over. "Long time no see," Jim said.

"Yeah, long time. Been pretty busy." Actually, he'd kept away since that winter night when he and Carol had their last drink before she flew back to Minnesota to care for her ailing father. A month or so later, he'd received the letter. She was staying, had gotten a job in the local hospital (Carol was a nurse), she was sorry. Paul had wondered if she'd hooked up with the old high school boyfriend that she'd told him about. Well, it didn't matter. She wasn't coming back.

Jim had brought him a whiskey sour. "So you remembered my drink?"

"Sure. You and Carol had them all the time. You hear from her?"

"Yeah. She's not coming back."

Jim shrugged. "Well, we didn't figure she was. She was really kind of a Midwestern girl, wasn't she?"

"*I suppose so." He tasted the drink, icy cold, good.

"How've you been?"

"Okay," Paul lied. Since Carol had left he'd been miserable.

"Still at that ad agency?"

"Yeah, even got a promotion. Been working hard. A big campaign."

"That's good. Keep your mind occupied." It hadn't kept him from thinking about Carol.

175

Another customer had come in, one of the regulars. Jim went down the bar to serve him. Paul looked into his drink. It couldn't help but remind him of all the times he'd come in here with Carol. Maybe coming back was a mistake. Then someone else came in, a girl, and sat a stool away from him. Jim came over to the girl and said, "Hi, Maggie. How you doing?"

The girl said, "I'm hot. Give me something cold." She was a petite girl with dark hair and eyes, attractive, nice legs. Paul smiled to himself at how she was almost the exact opposite of tall blonde Carol.

Jim gave her a whiskey sour. "Hey," he said. "You work in an ad agency, downtown, don't you?"

"Yeah. Why?"

"Paul here works in one, too. Maggie Miles, this is Paul Weiss. Maggie's out here from Chicago."

They said "Hi" and told each other where they worked. It turned out they were at different ad agencies but in the same building. "Small world," said Paul. "I've probably seen you. I'm in research. What about you?"

"I just started a few weeks ago. I'm only a secretary. But I want to get into the art department. I have my degree in art."

"Couldn't find an art job in Chicago?"

"I didn't look. I didn't want to stay in Chicago. To tell the truth, I broke up with my old high school boy friend and wanted to get away. An old story, right?"

"Yeah." Just like Carol. Only now Carol might have gotten back with hers. "Think you'll ever go back there, to Chicago?"

She smiled, an attractive smile that brightened her face. "Back to the snow and ice? Not a chance."

"I know what you mean. I came out here from New York. So, have you met anyone in San Francisco yet?" It was presumptuous to ask, but he felt he had to.

"You mean a guy? I told you, I've only been here a few weeks."

"I forgot." A few more people had come in and sat at the bar. Almost without thinking Paul stood up, took both of their drinks and led her to a table in the back, just as he'd always done with Carol. They sat down and he said, "This is better."

"Yes, much."

"Do you come in here often?"

"A few times. I live pretty close by. I like it in here. It's usually dark and quiet. And Jim's friendly. Tonight I just felt I had to get out of my apartment. It was so hot."

"Yeah, I felt the same way."

"Have you known Jim for long?"

"About a year, I guess. My place is also pretty close. Are you ready for another drink?"

"I think so." She reached into her purse but Paul said, "It's okay, I have it. Call it a welcome drink."

"All right."

Paul walked to the bar and ordered two more whiskey sours. "How's it going?" asked Jim.

"Fine."

"Maggies's a nice girl."

"She seems so."

Jim waited, as if expecting Paul to say something more, then handed him the drinks.

Back at the table, Maggie said, "Thanks. These are good."

"So, have you had a chance to see much of the city?"

"A little. I've been to Golden Gate Park. It's nice there. And I like the museums."

"How about Tommy's Joynt? Everyone goes there." Tommy's Joynt was a San Francisco institution, a hof-brau famous for its roast beef, beers from all over the world and Irish coffee. The last time he and Carol had gone there they'd shared a table with some Irish guys. It had been a cold foggy night, the usual San Francisco weather, not at all like tonight, and one of the Irish guys had bought them all Irish coffees. They'd had a good time.

"I've heard of it but no, I haven't been there."

"You have to sometime. How about Sausalito and Tiburon? Over the Golden Gate Bridge in Marin."

"No, I don't have a car. I'm saving up to buy one."

"No one in New York has a car so when I came out here I didn't even know how to drive. I took three lessons and got my license. I think the driving school had some kind of deal with the DMV. I bought an old Chevy and practiced in Golden Gate Park. It's a good thing you weren't out here then or you life would have been in danger."

She laughed. "Do you know how to drive now?"

"I think so. I try to stay away from those hills though."

"I'll remember that."

Paul looked at his watch. "Well, I better be getting back. What about you? I can give you a ride."

"No, I'm only a few blocks away. I'll just finish my drink and walk back. Thanks again for the drink, by the way."

"My pleasure."

As Paul went out he saw Jim look at him and mouth the word "Well." Paul shook his head and went out the door. It was still hot and there was a breathless feeling in the air as if something momentous was about to happen. He knew that some San Francisco natives called this "earthquake weather." Was an earthquake coming? It was possible. He took a few steps toward his car, then turned abruptly and went back into the bar. He went straight to the table where Maggie was still sitting. She looked up at him, seeming a little startled.

"Look," he said. "You really have to go to Tommy's Joynt. How about Saturday?"

She hesitated at first, then said, "All right. Fine."

Paul wrote down her name and phone number on a napkin Well, it wasn't as momentous as an earthquake, but it was something. For the first time since Carol had left, he'd be going out with a girl.

The Talking Computer
(Winamop)

The flu that had swept through our retirement community claimed me as a victim. I had a sore throat, stuffy nose and a foggy head. I'd just had a coughing spell that had jolted me awake. It was only seven AM but I felt too uncomfortable to go back to sleep. I slid quietly out of bed so as not to awaken my wife and went out, first to the bathroom and then to what was known as my computer room (a small second bedroom).

It's my habit first thing in the morning to turn on my computer, check my overnight e-mails and look at the stock market numbers and early news. I might mention here that although I'm retired I'm not completely idle as every month I write two columns for a senior newspaper, one called "Favorite Restaurants" and one called "Observations." I also write short stories for several online magazines.

The computer came on and a woman's voice said, "Hello, Martin. You're up early this morning."

I was startled, then I remembered that my son, who's a software engineer, had given my computer the capacity to speak. "Good morning," I said. "I have this flu and it woke me up."

"You don't sound too good. You must take care of yourself." The voice sounded concerned. My son had done a good job.

"I wanted to check my e-mail," I said.

"I know. You have an e-mail from an online publication with the strange name of "winamop." The new issue is out and you have a story in it. The other e-mails were all spam. I've deleted them."

"Oh. Okay. I also wanted to . . ."

"Check the financial markets. The Dow Jones is down 112 points. A bad jobs report. But your mutual fund is even and your bonds are up a little."

"Good. What about the news?"

"The usual. California has a budget deficit, the presidential candidates are smearing each other and Greece is in trouble."

"You're very efficient. I really don't feel up to it but I have to write my two columns for the senior paper today."

"I've scanned your last few "Observations" and have written a new one that is similar. I believe you'll find it satisfactory."

"Wow! You *are* efficient. But I still have to do the "Favorite Restaurants.""

"Ill scan the notes you've made and give you an outline."

"That's great. I'll come back after breakfast and finish it."

"I shall wait for your return. Do not forget to take your medications."

I went into the kitchen. My wife had gotten up and was preparing breakfast. She asked me how I was feeling.

"I had a bad night, but I'm feeling a little better now."

"Don't forget to take your pills."

"I won't. The computer has already reminded me."

"The computer?"

"Yes, Chris has given it a voice capacity. It's already done my Observations column for me and is going to do an outline for Favorite Restaurants. It's great."

"Chris? Have you forgotten that he's in Ireland?"

I thought, Yes, he is. How could that be? Then the fog in my head seemed to clear. "I wonder if I've been dreaming?"

After breakfast, I went back to the computer. I looked at it. It stared impassively back at me. I said, in a low voice, "Hello." The computer said nothing. I guess I had been dreaming, or doing some wishful thinking. Well, it would have been nice. Maybe in a few years . . . But if it had been a dream, it had been very vivid. Maybe I could make a story out of it.

Rajah
(Winamop)

When Douglas Farnsworth was a boy he'd been small, very smart, wore glasses and liked to read books. Like many boys of this kind he'd had few friends. But he did have an imaginary playmate, a big tiger named Rajah. Douglas's favorite pastime was to read books like "Kidnapped" and "Treasure Island," sitting on the floor, propped up against Rajah. He'd relate the details of the plots to Rajah, who'd listen gravely, nodding his head every now and then. Douglas's mother and father didn't like the idea of an imaginary tiger but Douglas seemed to be so devoted to him that they finally gave in and accepted Rajah, reasoning that this was just a phase. His father said, "The way Douglas talks to him I could almost swear he was actually there."

"I know," said his mother. "When I clean up his bedroom, I sometimes think I see a tail disappearing around a corner."

Also, like many boys of his kind, Douglas had been a natural target of school bullies but something in his manner, perhaps the assurance of having a large tiger as his friend, put off potential bullies and he'd had a relatively pleasant childhood. There'd been one exception, when Douglas was in third grade. A boy named Wilbur Scruggs, who lived with his aunt and uncle in a trailer camp, began to pick on him and one day told Douglas to watch it, he was going to catch him after school and beat him up. Douglas gave this information to Rajah and said he planned to hit Wilbur first and at least get in one good blow. He never got a chance to put his plan in action because the next day Wilbur disappeared. A search was made but nothing was found except a shoe that may or may not have belonged to Wilbur. The aunt and uncle weren't especially interested and the search was soon ended. Douglas never saw Wilbur again.

As might be expected with someone who liked to read so much, Douglas gravitated to literature in college and eventually became a professor of English. Here too there was one obstacle, an older professor named Philip Crenshaw who'd taken a dislike to him and who was blocking Douglas's path to getting tenure. By this time Douglas had married and had two children, a boy and a girl. The imaginary tiger had of course long since evaporated, but the family did have a cat that Douglas had named Rajah II. On the eve of the meeting that would decide whether or not Douglas would be granted tenure Professor Crenshaw was found on campus, scratched and disheveled, his eyes crazed and babbling about a monster that had attacked him. He was taken to a sanitarium to recover. Without Crenshaw's presence at the meeting, Douglas was granted tenure. He sometimes wondered about what might have happened to Crenshaw but eventually told himself that further speculation was pointless and that some things should just be accepted.

As the years passed, Douglas's life continued to be pleasant but with the collapse of values and an increasingly permissive society acts of violence increased and his college was not immune to them. A disgruntled student invaded a classroom and shot and killed his teacher and several other students before turning his gun on himself. A lab assistant killed a co-worker, a woman who'd broken up with him. Student protests were common. Most recently, a series of robberies had taken place at homes on and around the campus, young people on drugs who took whatever they could get and routinely trashed everything else.

It was evening. Douglas was in his study writing. He heard the sound of glass breaking and had just stood up behind his desk when two young men in masks burst into the room. Both held guns. Douglas was glad that his wife was away, visiting her mother. "Hello, Professor," the smaller one said. He held a gun. "Thought we'd pay you a little visit."

"What do you want?"

The young man looked around. "Nice house," he said. "Where do you keep your money?"

"I have some in my wallet, but it's not much."

"You must have some more somewhere."

"I really don't."

The larger one stepped forward and hit Douglas across the face with his gun. "We're not kidding around," he said.

"All right. I do have a safe in my bedroom. It's upstairs. I'll give you the combination. You're welcome to take whatever you want."

"That's the spirit, Professor," said the smaller one. "Keep your eye on him," he told his confederate. "I'll go up and take a look." He went up the stairs.

"You have any drugs in the house?" the larger one asked.

"Just the medicines I take. I . . ."

A loud crash came from upstairs, then a terrified scream.

"What the hell?" said the robber. He ran up the stairs. Douglas heard more loud noises from above, then the two young men came running down the stairs, ran through the study and out of the house. Douglas picked up his phone and dialed 911.

It was late when the police finally left. First, they wanted to know if Douglas was all right after being hit in the face. He assured them he was fine and didn't have to go to the hospital. Then they wanted to know if he had any idea what had so frightened the two robbers. Douglas told them he didn't know. "Well," said the lead policeman, "they must have been pretty scared because one of them dropped his gun. We should be able to identify it and trace it to him. I think the crime wave we've been having will be over soon."

Douglas was very tired when he finally went into his bedroom. His cat, Rajah IV, was sitting on the bed. "Well, that was quite a night," Douglas said. The cat nodded. "What do you think happened?" he asked. The cat appeared to contemplate this question for a moment but then just gave him the complacent look that cats sometime assume and said nothing. As in the case of Professor Crenshaw's mysterious "monster," Douglas concluded that speculation was pointless and that some things should just be accepted.

The Girl (?) Next Door
(Winamop)

Wait a minute. What was going on here? I'd taken the beautiful mysterious woman next door to dinner, having finally gotten up the nerve to ask her, and now, at her door, had just given her a tentative good-night kiss. This was inevitably the end of any date, (and these had been few and far between) I'd ever had. But the lovely Selena was kissing me back, hard, and incredibly, she was pulling me through the doorway. Selena's dark eyes glistened and her perfect breasts pressed against my chest. Before I knew what was happening, we were in her bedroom.

Let me go back a little. I'm just an average guy. I'm 35 years old, at least ten years older than I'd say Selena was. I make a decent living as a researcher for a brokerage firm, but I'm not rich by any means. I'm certainly not good-looking. And Selena, she was the most beautiful woman I'd ever seen. She'd moved in about a month ago. She'd knocked on my door several times, asking me to explain how things in her place worked, the dishwasher, the air-conditioner, even her coffee maker.

Naturally, I was entranced by her. To my amazement, she seemed interested in me. She wanted to know all about my job. She asked me questions about the stock market and how it worked. What made some stocks go up and some go down? How did I know which companies were good buys and which were not? How was the market regulated? Could someone manipulate it? I found myself spending two or three evenings a week in her apartment.

Did I say she was mysterious as well as lovely? She told me nothing about herself. When I asked she evaded my questions and said she'd tell me later. Judging from her apartment's furnishings she must have had money, but she didn't seem to have a job. I never saw any evidence that she did any cooking. I was curious about her but that didn't matter. It was enough that she was beautiful and that she appeared to like me. There was only one flaw in our relationship, my cat Mickey didn't like her. The first time Selena was in my place she tried to pet Mickey, who uncharacteristically scratched her. It looked like a deep scratch, but Selena said it was nothing. When I looked, there was no sign of a scratch at all. That was strange, but I didn't think anything about it, not at the time.

* * *

If this was another kind of story I'd now have to describe in intimate detail the first night I spent at Selena's. Suffice it to say, it exceeded even my wildest expectations. One thing was surprising. I'm not a great lover; I know the basics and that's about all. With her fantastic looks, I expected that Selena had had many lovers and was experienced in all the ins and outs of sex. But she didn't seem to be any more knowledgeable than myself. As she had with my work, she asked a lot of questions. She also read books and I found out that she was a fast learner.

Selena was in fact curious about many things. Her apartment was filled with books, the ones about sex being the latest additions. She had books about world history, science, economics, climate and, surprisingly, physics. She also had a laptop, on which she spent a lot of time, but she never let me look at it. It contained her private thoughts, she said.

As I've mentioned, I saw no signs in Selena's apartment that she ever did any cooking. After I came home from work, I usually made dinner for us. Selena and my cat Mickey had arrived at a truce. Mickey kept her distance and Selena made no further attempt to befriend her. It was clear that Mickey remained suspicious.

If my first night with Selena was fantastic, the month that followed was an idyll. Then after dinner one night she told me that in a short time she'd be leaving. "What?" I said. "Where are you going?"

"To a place far away."

"Why?"

"My time here has come to an end. It's time for me to return home."

"I'll come with you."

"I'm afraid that's not possible."

I was devastated. "Will you come back?"

"In time, but then things will be changed."

"Changed? How?"

She smiled. "You'll see. Now come, let's enjoy the present."

Selena kissed me and soon one thing led to another. As I've said, she was a fast learner with regard to sex and for that night I forgot everything else.

*   *   *

When I returned from work the next day everything Selena had in my apartment was gone. I knocked on the door to her apartment; there was no answer. I went back downstairs and found Mr. Jensen, the super. Selena had left that morning, he told me. I said I might have left some things in her place; he let me have her key. The apartment was completely empty, no books and of course no laptop.

I returned to my place, a pain in my heart. I don't know how long I just sat there. I do know that it became dark outside. Finally, I roused myself. I got the flash drive on which I'd downloaded the contents of Selena's laptop when she'd been sleeping the previous night and put it into my computer. A number of files appeared. I opened some and they were in a language I didn't know. Then I saw a file with my name heading it. I opened the file. Part was in the same unintelligible language, but there were some sections in English. I read: "easy to seduce . . . knows a considerable amount about the stock market but little else . . . afraid he's fallen in love, as humans on Earth say, . . ." I read some more; it was in the same vein.

I was incredulous, but then I wasn't. Of course Selena wasn't really interested in me. I wondered if she'd been placed next door to me because of my stock market knowledge and my innocence in all other matters. It occurred to me that I should inform someone about Selena, the government maybe, but they would just think I was crazy. Maybe I was because I still yearned for her. She'd said she'd return in time. I wondered when, and I wondered who or what else would come with her.

The Magic Racket
(Clever Magazine)

Paul Lerner was leaving his swim and tennis club when he noticed the broken tennis racket stuffed into the trash can just outside the entrance. At least he assumed it was broken; otherwise, why was it in there with the trash? Curious, he pulled it out. It looked expensive and seemed okay, but when he sighted down the handle he could see that the frame was slightly bent, as if someone had smashed it on the ground. If that's what had happened, he could sympathize because the way he'd been playing lately he'd sometimes felt like doing the same thing with his own racket. He hefted the slightly bent racket again and thought, What the hell, I might as well keep it, just in case I do smash my own racket; I could probably use it for a set or two anyway . . .

Paul, who was in his thirties, had only seriously taken up tennis a few months ago, after he and his wife had joined the club, mainly so that their two young sons could have a place to swim. Three of his new neighbors—Ernie, Mort and Bob—belonged to the club and were tennis players so they'd invited him to join them. They usually played Saturday mornings. In a short time, Paul was competitive with the others, but felt he should be playing even better. He considered himself a pretty good athlete, he'd played baseball in high school, but he couldn't seem to get beyond a certain level.

Sometimes he thought that if he could play with the club's better players he'd improve his game. But the better players, as happened in most clubs, were a clique who played among themselves on the first three courts, the ones next to the clubhouse, and looked down on hackers such as his foursome, who always played on one of the end courts.

Three weeks later, a string in Paul's regular racket broke in the middle of a set. Well, he thought, now was as good a time as any to try out the other racket and see if he could play with it. He was playing with Bob against Ernie and Mort and serving to Ernie, usually a consistent returner, at 15-40. He served, not very hard, but just as Ernie prepared to hit the ball it took a funny hop to the right and Ernie completely missed it. Paul's next serve took a hop to the left with the same result. Ernie managed to get his racket on Paul's next two serves, both of which also swerved crazily, but couldn't get them back over the net. "Hey, what are you putting on your serve," Ernie called.

Paul looked down at the racket. "I don't know," he said. The pattern continued for the rest of the set. Everything Paul hit either hopped to the right or left or skidded or took a crazy bounce. Most of the time the shot couldn't be returned. Paul and Ernie won the set 6-2. Following their usual routine, they rotated partners. Paul won the next set playing with Mort 6-0, then, playing with Bob, the weakest of their foursome, won again 6-3. Paul's served more aces than he had in all of their previous sets. Gathering confidence with his new racket, he also hit more winners than he ever had. After their last set, when they were sitting on the club's patio having their customary beers, the other three marveled at Paul's sudden prowess. "It must be that new racket," Ernie said.

"Maybe he's been taking lessons in secret," said Bob.

"You'll be playing with the big boys next," said Mort.

Paul shrugged and said, "It's probably a fluke. We'll see next week."

                                    *   *   *

But the next week, as Paul got used to his new racket, his play was even better . . . That afternoon Paul was at the club's pool with his wife Sally and their two boys when Ken Beasley, one of the top tennis players, came up to him and asked if he could make a fourth the following Saturday as one of their regulars would be out of town. "I noticed you playing this morning," Beasley told him. "You looked pretty good, a lot better than those other guys."

"Sure," said Paul. "I have a new racket and it's helped my game."

"Okay. See you at nine o'clock."

When Beasley left, Sally said, "I thought you had a regular game with Bob, Mort and Ernie on Saturday morning."

Paul was annoyed. "This is my chance to move up to real competition. They can get somebody to fill in for me."

                                    *   *   *

The next Saturday Paul met Ken Beasley at the club. They were to play doubles against two of the club's other top players, Scott Trimble and Mark Harris. They were on court one. Paul was nervous as they warmed up and then started to play. He thought to himself that these guys hit the ball harder than he was used to and that they knew how to play at the net. Also, the crazy spins and hops he was able to put on the ball with his new racket, didn't completely baffle them. Still, they had a hard time returning his serves and his shots and Beasley, who also knew how to cover the net, had an easy time putting away their weak returns. They won the first set 6-4 and then the second set 7-5.

The next few Saturdays they had the same foursome, alternating partners. Paul didn't have the skills of the other three, but, with the aid of his racket, managed to hold his own. Another thing Paul noticed was that the others were intensively competitive. They didn't play recreational tennis; they played for blood. Mark Harris was the worst. When he missed a shot he cursed and sometimes threw his racket. When his partner missed a shot he yelled at him. Paul didn't like being his partner and because he was nervous about being yelled at he'd press and play below his game.

The final blow-up came in their last set on the last Saturday of the month. Paul was Mark Harris's partner and was serving at 5-6; he had to hold service or they'd lose the set. He aced Trimble to go ahead 15-0, but Beasley, who'd adjusted pretty well to his crazy bounces, his back a winner for 15-15. Then Trimble hit back a weak return of serve and Harris put it away for 30-15. Beasley timed Paul's next serve, hit a good return and they rallied until Paul put the ball in the net, 30-30. Harris glared at him. Then Trimble again hit a weak return of serve but this time Harris misplayed it and hit long, 30-40, break point. Paul's first serve to Beasley went into the net for a fault. Harris looked back at him and yelled, "You better not double fault." Paul tried to put some extra spin on his second serve, Beasley's return was weak and they won the point, and then the next two points for the game. Then in the tiebreaker they lost 8-6 as Paul couldn't return one of Beasley's hard serves. Harris picked up the ball, smashed it into the net and stalked off the court.

The other two told Paul not to worry, he'd played okay and Harris would get over it. Maybe, thought Paul, but would he? He'd wanted to improve his game but did he want to approach tennis as if he was going to war every weekend? It was a lot more fun when he was playing with his neighbors. He guessed that at heart he was a recreational player. Besides, he wasn't really that good a player. It was the bent racket that created all those funny bounces that had made him seem that much better. He hadn't really improved his game.

The next weekend he approached the guys—Ernie, Bob and Mort—and said he'd like to get back in a foursome with them.

"What's the matter?" asked Ernie. "Those big guys too tough for you."

"No, I was able to hold my own. They just take the game too seriously. It's no fun playing with them."

"Hey," said Bob. "We heard about Mark Harris throwing his racket at you."

"He didn't throw his racket. He just got mad."

"What do you say, guys, should we let Paul back in?" said Mort.

"Only if he buys the first round of beers," said Ernie.

"Yeah," said Bob. "And if he promises not to play with that funny racket any more."

"It's a deal," said Paul.

So Paul went back to playing tennis for fun and gradually, using a regular racket, his game did improve. But he didn't throw away the bent racket. There'd be a singles tournament on Labor Day and maybe he'd enter and maybe he'd get to play against Mark Harris and just maybe . . .

The Next-to-Last Station
(Hackwriters)

Five years before, on Paul Lerner's 75th birthday, his wife Sally had insisted on celebrating the event by having a big party in the ballroom of the Northern California retirement community where they'd lived for ten years. Paul hadn't wanted such a big fuss made but hadn't objected too strongly. After all, he'd thought, he'd survived three-quarters of a century in this turbulent era and that was something of an achievement. But in the interval he'd had several health problems and felt all of his 80 years old. All he wanted to do on his 80th birthday was to spend the day restfully and peacefully. Of course, he told himself, this was too much to hope for and sure enough, his oldest son Nick had invited him and Sally to come over for the afternoon, for "just a little family party." Paul suspected that Nick's wife Maria had been the instigator; she liked to throw "little parties" in their large over-priced home. As it was a chance to see their ten-year old grandson Scott, they couldn't refuse.

Nick and Maria had bought their house a few years ago, before the housing bubble had burst in Sacramento, as it had nationwide. Paul had been afraid that, like many others, they wouldn't be able to pay the sizeable monthly mortgage. But Nick, who worked for the State of California, as Paul had done years before, had risen to a high position in his department and Maria had obtained a high-paying job in a non-profit agency. Paul thought his son, now in his early 40's, had turned out to be a good-looking man; at six feet, he was three inches taller than his father; he was athletic (he worked out daily), outgoing and self-confident. Paul was sure that the bureaucratic inanities that had so annoyed him just rolled off Nick. He was also good at office politics, which Paul had never been. Maria was an attractive woman, also tall and self-confident, always well turned-out. The two, Paul considered, made a handsome couple.

Paul let Sally drive them to Nick and Maria's house. The day before for some reason his right knee had stiffened up and he could hardly bend it. It was one of those things that happened with age. When they arrived, Scott was the first one at the door. "Grandad," he said. "Happy birthday. Come look at my trains." Scott was a tall, slender boy, with his mother's fair hair and blue eyes. He'd gone through various stages in his enthusiasms, first with a cartoon character, Thomas Train, then with Spiderman, then Batman and now, as Paulo recalled, with some kind of Ninja super hero. But he'd also gone back to trains, only now with rather expensive trains on a track he'd set up in his room.

"Let Grandma and Grandad sit down first," said Nick, coming into the hallway. They went into the living room, where a long table had been covered with dishes arranged buffet-style: lunch meats, cheeses, fruits, crackers and dips, Maria's idea of a light meal, thought Paul. As usual, she greeted him with a kiss, took his coat, then sat him down in an overstuffed chair, much like a throne. She would also have brought him whatever he wanted to eat, but he joined the others in lining up and filling his plate. While he didn't mind a little pampering, he could still get his own food. Once seated they ate and exchanged news of what they'd been doing in the month since they'd last been together. There wasn't much news on his side, thought Paul, just a few visits to the doctor, which he didn't see the need of telling them. On their side, they'd discovered a great new restaurant. Scott was doing well in school. They were thinking of taking him on a cruise that summer; families cruising together was becoming a popular thing to do.

While they talked, Paul thought back to when Nick was born, their first baby, three years after they'd married. Marriage, then buying a house when Sally became pregnant, then the baby. All stages in the journey of life. The last stage, he supposed, was old age. After they'd finished eating, Maria brought out a cake, his birthday cake. Fortunately, she'd put eight, not eighty, candles on it. They sang "Happy Birthday" to him. Paul hadn't thought he'd still be hungry but the cake was good. Then Paul was given a birthday present, a gift card to a book store. Paul had told them he didn't want any gifts but he thanked them; as he got older he was trying to read more. After all that, he felt himself getting sleepy. He told Sally that maybe they'd better be getting home.

"You have to look at my trains," cried Scott.

"Oh, yes." Paul stood up, his right knee causing him to wince. "Let's have a look."

Paul saw that Scott now had two trains, one passenger and one freight. The track was a figure-eight. Scott also had three or four stations set up, buildings, people, trees. He showed Paul how he operated the two trains at once. When the trains passed each other, each gave a loud whistle. As with his son Nick, looking at his grandson Paul saw two Scotts, the baby he'd welcomed into the world and now the ten-year old boy, before you knew it, he'd be the young man going off to college. Paul stayed as long as he could, admiring his grandson's trains. When they left, he shook hands with Nick, then he suddenly felt impelled to give him a hug, and then he gave Scott a hug.

When they were home, Paul went to his chair, leaned back, put up his feet, and fell asleep. He had a dream. He was riding in a train. A lot of other people were on it; old people, like himself. He looked out the window. The landscape was green, the sun glinting off trees, then it became gray. The train stopped. The conductor came by. "Are we at the end of the line?" asked Paul.

"No," said the conductor. "There's one more stop, but you get off here. This is the next-to-last station."

Paul abruptly awoke. Usually, he couldn't remember his dreams but this one was still distinct in his mind. The next-to-last station. Old age. Of course he knew what the last stop was, the station at the end of everyone's life journey. He was getting close to it, but he wasn't there quite yet.

The next day the pain in Paul's right knee went away as suddenly as it had came. At breakfast, he said to Sally, "Our anniversary is in three months. What do you say we go on a cruise?"

Sally looked up, surprised. They hadn't done any real traveling in the last few years. "Do you feel up to it?"

"To tell the truth, I'm not sure, but as long as I'm still here let's take a chance. The last station will be coming up soon."

"The last station?"

"Never mind."

The Hitch-hiker: A Memory
(Hackwriters)

It was 1946. He was 17, a high school senior. He'd been let off on the main street of a small Midwestern town. It was mid-afternoon. He hadn't eaten since the morning. He saw a diner, went in and sat down at the counter. He set the gym bag carrying his things down on the floor. The waitress behind the counter came over. She was in her forties, with dyed blonde hair and a tired face. The apple pie in the case looked good. He ordered a slice and a glass of milk. She brought them over.

He was hungry. "Hmmm, this pie tastes good," he said.

"You're not from around here, are you?" the waitress said.

"No, just passing through."

"Where are you from?"

"New York. That's where I'm going."

"Where are you coming from?"

"Idaho. I worked in the Forestry Service over the summer."

"Idaho? That's a long ways. How come you went way out there?"

"A friend of mine told me about it. They paid a dollar an hour, time and a half on Saturday. And you had your room and board so everything you made was clear. It was a good deal."

"Hope you didn't spend it all on some girl friend."

"No girl friend. There was really nothing to spend it on. The nearest town was about 30 miles away."

An older man had sat down at the counter. "Hi, Mary," he said. "Cup of coffee." He looked down at the gym bag. "You hitch-hiking?" he asked.

"Yes."

"Have any trouble?"

"Not yet. Well, a little, in Montana, when I started out. The guy was drunk so I asked him to stop and I got out, on a winding road in the mountains. Luckily, a guy stopped, a school teacher visiting his sister, and he drove me all the way to Iowa."

"That was lucky," the man said. "A lot of soldier boys on the road; people like to give them rides. Were you in the service?"

"No, too young."

"He was in the Forestry Service," said Mary.

"That so? Fight any fires?"

"No. We had training but there was a lot of rain so no fires."

"He's going back to New York," said Mary. "I bet he has a girl back there."

"No, not really."

"He's blushing."

Give him another slice of that pie," the man said. "I'll get his bill."

"Thanks." When he finished they wished him good luck.

He walked down Main Street, a gas station, a general store, a clothing store, a few other shops. People were moving up and down the street, going about their business. He came to a few houses. He could see people through the windows and suddenly he felt a pang of loneliness. When he came to the point where the road led out of town he put down his gym bag and started to wait for cars to come along.

The feeling of loneliness persisted; everyone else in that little town has his or her place and he was just a stranger, on the outside. But it wasn't too bad. He knew he wasn't really all by himself. His mother was waiting for his return, although she didn't know he was hitch-hiking; she thought he was taking a bus. She'd make a big fuss over him. Then he was going off to college. He had a scholarship that would pay for his tuition. He would be working on campus for his room and board. He hoped the money he'd saved over he summer would cover his books and other expenses.

He waited. The last ride he'd had was a short one, just two towns over. He wanted another long ride, like the one he'd gotten in Montana. It was mid-afternoon. The landscape was flat. The sky was a pale blue. The sun looked fiery. It was hot. Nothing like New York City, but then he'd become used to different settings, even the national forest in which he'd worked. And to different people. Usually, they were nice, like those two in the diner. Again, he felt lonely and small, just a slight figure in this flat land that seemed to stretch forever. Sooner or later though the right car would come along and he'd be on his way again. Until then he was by himself, alone; but something else, he was, for that moment, free.

Violet
(Clever Magazine)

I was in my twenties when I transferred from San Francisco to Sacramento to get a promotion in the State's giant Health Department. I became a section supervisor and as such had a lot of meetings with other section supervisors working on the same programs. On one of my trips back from such a meeting I noticed a new clerk-typist, pardon me, an office technician in the State's new jargon. I noticed her because she was very pretty. She had long brown hair, nice features and wore a tight sweater emphasizing her bosom. I went over and introduced myself. She told me her name was Violet. She'd come to Sacramento from a little town near Fresno.

"It's hot here," I said, "but probably won't be as hot as Fresno."

"Did you say it'll be hotter here than Fresno?"

"No, *not* as hot."

"Oh."

We talked a little more and I asked her to lunch for later in the week. She accepted. When the day came I took her to the Capitol cafeteria, which was a cut above the ones in the State buildings. I asked how she liked her job and she said her section chief was a nice guy. She asked me if I liked my job and I said I did and that my boss was also a nice guy. "Did you say he wasn't such a nice guy?" she asked.

"No, he *is.*"

"Oh."

Despite a few little misunderstandings like this we got along well. She liked Sacramento. She'd found an apartment downtown with another girl who also worked for the State. They thought there was a lot to do in what was a big city compared to her home town. We walked back through Capitol Park. Although it was summer it wasn't too warm. The roses were out in full bloom and the park's squirrels were scampering around. Violet wore a light dress and looked very pretty. I asked her to dinner and she said that would be nice.

I continued to see Vi, as she was usually called, through the summer. She wasn't exactly a mental giant but she'd gone to community college. She liked reading, although mostly romances. She also liked romantic movies. She made some astute remarks about working for the State, like how she spent a lot of time typing memos that didn't seem to accomplish anything. Every now and then she still misinterpreted something I said. I'd comment on a movie we'd seen to the effect that it would have been better if an hour shorter and she'd take it that I'd said an hour longer. Also, whenever I'd comment on the weather, saying it was really hot that day or not as hot as usual for a Sacramento summer she'd take it that I'd said just the opposite.

Our dating went the usual course that dating did in those days. When I took her back to her apartment I'd kiss her good night. Several times after a dinner or movie I got her to come up to my apartment and we reached the point where we "made out" pretty hot and heavy on my sofa, but she'd proceed no further. Also, I didn't like to ask her to my place too often as it was so small and the furniture that came with it was so shabby. I decided that she was a fairly innocent girl. I didn't think she realized how attractive she was and how provocative her tight sweaters were. When all was said and done, she was really good-looking and all of my fellow State workers who knew I was taking her out were envious of me.

Still, as summer moved into fall I found that her misinterpretations of my remarks were getting on my nerves. I had one or two discussions with her about this and she said she was sorry, she'd listen more carefully. The next day, however, the same thing would happen. The worst thing was when she told me that her roommate was going out of town for the weekend and I got the impression that I could come over and we'd get beyond the heavy making out, finally. When I arrived at her door, full of anticipation, I found to my surprise that her roommate was still there and Vi said she'd thought I'd told her I wanted to see more of the roommate, not that I'd be happy to see no more of her, as I'd said.

At about the same time, another girl came into our office, an analyst who'd graduated from UC Berkeley. She wasn't nearly as pretty as Vi (few girls were) but she was smart and funny. I could talk to her easily and she understood everything I said exactly as I said it. I decided it was time to break off with Vi. The question was how to do it. She was such a nice girl I couldn't hurt her. I'd have to ease out gently. I began to make excuses for not seeing her and our dates became fewer. I was still at a loss as to how to make a complete break when I hired an analyst for my section. His name was Gordon Jones, a recent graduate of Sac State, a good-looking kid and a hard worker, always wanting to please.

One morning I asked Gordon to bring me some birth figures for the last few years. I added, "Bring me 2005-2006, too." A few minutes later he was back. "Did you say you wanted the 2005-2006 figures or you didn't want them?"

"I said I *wanted* them." Hmmm, I thought. To make sure, that afternoon I gave Gordon a spreadsheet of figures to calculate. "Oh, yeah," I said, "Make up a graph, also." Again, he was back in a few minutes. "Uh, did you say you wanted a graph or you didn't want a graph?"

"I *did* want a graph." That clinched it. I picked up my phone and called Vi. "Hi, I said. "Look, how about lunch tomorrow? I have someone I want you to meet. A nice young guy who just started in my section. You'll like him. You and he have a lot in common."